We're Bitches

MICHAEL POLILLO

Copyright © 2019 Michael Polillo

This book is a work of fiction. The product of the author's imagination.

All rights reserved. No part of this book may be used or reproduced in any manner whatsoever without permission.

First Printing, 2019

ISBN-13: 9 781 698 554 099

Cover art assets free for commercial use through pixabay by:

christels – Wolf's head

skeeze – Beach background

adamkontor – Bikini body

Contents

Chapter 1	pg. 1
Chapter 2	pg. 9
Chapter 3	pg. 17
Chapter 4	pg. 26
Chapter 5	pg. 33
Chapter 6	pg. 42
Chapter 7	pg. 51
Chapter 8	pg. 61
Chapter 9	pg. 69
Chapter 10	pg. 82
Chapter 11	pg. 91
Chapter 12	pg. 100
Chapter 13	pg. 107
Chapter 14	pg. 115

But, there, you can't trust wolves no more nor women.

Bram Stoker, *Dracula*

CHAPTER 1

The full moon was giving plenty of light to the beach down below. The Atlantic ocean was softly crashing in the night. Crabs scuttled to and fro and they were the main entertainment for the beach's guests. They moved freely and without any care as to being seen. The night was theirs to enjoy. This was Holborn, New Jersey. A southern shore town crowded with tourists who visited to forget about life for awhile.

A small bonfire was burning in the sands. Surrounding it were four sitting figures. Two tents were pitched nearby while the people were basking in the warmth of the flames. Two women, two men. The figures were paired off and the couples embraced each other. They had been swimming all day between pick-up games of baseball and now they were enjoying the stillness of the night ocean. The first couple resembled each other. Both tall, both built, both with dark hair. The second couple were a stocky man and a short woman who couldn't look more different. Resembling each other or not, they had all been going on vacation together for the last five summers. And none of them had seen this many crabs on a beach at night before. There was always one in their line of sight no matter where they were staring. That is, when they weren't gazing at each other.

"Look at that one go," said the built man.

A palm sized crab was boogieing down the sands back into the water right across from where they were sitting. The short woman rose and rushed over to take a closer look. She bent down, scooped up the crab and brought it back to the fire. She held it from the back and it's claws pinched at empty air. One claw was three times larger than the other.

"What kind of crab is that?" said the stocky man.

"Fiddler. See its big claw? It resembles a fiddle," said the built man.

"The fuck's a fiddle?"

"A violin. Did you pay attention at all in school?"

"Oh I'm sorry. I didn't realize I was dealing with the king of animals and instruments. My apologies for asking," said the stocky man.

"The big claw means it's a male crab. Bet you didn't know that either."

The two women were admiring the fiddler while paying little attention to the men. Photos were snapped and selfies were taken.

"I don't know how you can grab those things like that," said the stocky man, "Be careful or you might lose a finger."

She brought the crab closer to her lover's face. It grabbed at his nose and he flinched backwards, laughing as he fell into the sand.

"You better be careful or you might lose an eye," she said.

The short woman placed the crab back on the beach and it headed to the water. They resumed their positions around the fire and with their respective partners.

"I wonder why are there so many of them out here tonight?" said the built woman.

"Maybe they like the moon. That's why we're out here, isn't it?" said the built man.

"I though we're out here because it was cheap to rent a spot for a tent," said the short woman.

"Before tonight I didn't even think it was legal to camp on Jersey beaches," said the stocky man.

"It isn't, that's why it was so cheap. I didn't pay a dime," said the built man.

"You mean we're out here illegally?"

"Hey it's either we camp illegally or wait until one of their rare camping events. Why did you think we're the only ones out here?"

"I figured most people were tired of beach camping."

"Most people don't want to break the law."

The two men continued to bicker once more as the women exchanged glances with each other. They were lucky to have made it through the day without them arguing. It was bound to happen at some point. Their discussion escalated into yelling about types of crabs, fines, and types of beer they enjoyed. It went on for a solid ten minutes before they were cut off by a howl that rang out in the night.

"Hey. Do you think you two can shut the fuck up for a minute?" said the short woman.

They closed their mouths and nodded.

"You two did hear that sound, right?" said the built woman.

"It was probably the wind. The beach at night always sounds like that. You're not scared of the wind now are you?" said the built man.

"What if it wasn't the wind though? What if there's something out there?" said the built woman.

"Like what? We're on a beach in Holborn. The worst thing here are those crabs that you were taking a selfie with," said the built man.

"I don't know, what if it's a wolf or something?" said the built woman.

"Hey now, even I know there's no wolves in New Jersey," said the stocky man.

"What if one escaped from the zoo? We're not too far from it. All I'm saying is it isn't impossible," said the short woman.

"There's no wolves at the Cape May zoo. The closest preserve place is hours by car," said the built man.

The women jumped into their man's arms and held them close. The men could see the fear in their eyes. Then another howl happened. All four of their bodies jolted and they nearly bounced to their feet.

"I'm telling you that's not the wind. There's something out there," said the built woman.

"Why would a wolf be hanging around a beach? There's barely anything for it to eat," said the stocky man.

"Yeah except all the tourists hanging around," said the short woman.

"We'd know if there were a wolf loose. That'd be some major news," said the stocky man.

"What if it's that weirdo Gordon trying to mess with us?" said the built woman.

The group couldn't see far away from the water. They had camped out near tall grass growing on the dunes. The blades provided great coverage for their tents to stay hidden. It unfortunately didn't let them see the roads from where they came. A third howl happened within a minute of the second and it seemed to be coming from the brush barely within sight of the fire. The women held a tight grip on the men. They could all feel each other shaking.

"Alright, enough talk. I'm not going to be scared by the wind. I'll go check it out and be back to tell you bitches there's nothing to be scare of," said the built man.

"Are you sure that's a good idea?" said the stocky man.

"If there's something out there then I'll call animal control and maybe they'll be so happy that they won't fine us for illegally camping here."

"Alright, be safe."

"You mean you're not coming with me?"

"Someone should stay with the women, right?"

They all nodded in agreement. The built man stood, kissed his lady and used his cell phone as a flashlight, walking into the grass. The others huddled around the fire and peeled their eyes, trying to keep a glimpse of the built man, but he was out of view before long. Still they kept their sight and hearing focused. The howling had stopped. There was no fourth call into the night. The trio stood after five minutes, wanting to go out there and find their friend. Their attention was pulled towards a thud in the sand only a few steps away. The stocky man ran over to it and bolted back. He had a sculpted arm in his hands with his return. A scream did ring out into the air. It wasn't theirs. The three tried to scream and found no strength to muster it. A shadow was running towards the fire, yelling and wailing. The flames revealed it to be the built man who was missing his arm. Blood was flooding out the empty socket and he was grasping at it trying to plug it with his fingers. He nearly made the camp before falling to his knees then face forward into the sand.

All three of them cried now. It was a moan mixed of pain and fear. The stocky man tried to console the women to little good. And little time passed before another thud was heard. They could see a new figure lit by the moonlight. Any outline of the figure would reveal it was on hind legs and covered in fur. It was clear that the women were half right. It was a lycanthrope staring them down. Better known as a werewolf to the common man. Flickers of flame showed flesh hanging from its mouth as it charged towards the group.

"What the fuck is that?" said the short woman.

"It doesn't matter, just run. Get out of here. Now," said the stocky man.

None of them were able to move. They were frozen as the creature closed in on them.

The stocky man readied himself with fists up. The werewolf ran at him first and he tried to jab at its face. The beast returned the punch with one of its own. The stocky man flew through the air, landing face down by one of the tents. The two women looked towards each other for comfort. They found none. The werewolf sprinted at the built woman with its claws out. She received a close look at the white covering the creature as one of its claws dug into her right thigh. Her fists hammered at the werewolf before she fell lifeless to the ground.

The short woman had ran to the fire to use as cover between her and the werewolf. She picked up a flaming stick and waved it in front of her. The werewolf broke the distance within three strides. It stood on the coals and the short woman swung her makeshift club. It broke on a furry arm and the other swung down into the woman's chest. She sunk into the fire while the air left her body.

The stocky man's spirit returned to him. He pushed himself off the sand and could see the werewolf standing around the campsite. It was fully lit by the fire now. It's clothes were shredded and hanging loosely on its furry white body. The man stood and the werewolf's head cocked at him. It's snout snarled and he dove into a tent. His hands rummaged quickly, lifting up bags, pillows, blankets until he found the baseball bat. He took a deep breath while planning his attack. The plan was cut short. A claw swept down into the tent, ripping open the ceiling, and exposing the stocky man to the beast. He swung the baseball bat down on the creature's head. It bounced off without as much as a hair being misplaced.

The werewolf heaved the man, carrying him back towards the fire. His arms flailed with little effect. He felt himself being lifted higher and higher. He could see the ground beneath him and then he could sense it. A claw grabbed him at the shoulders. Another held him at the groin. He felt his body twist and he shrieked as he found himself falling back into the sand. He looked up to see the brute holding his legs and taking bites out of them like baguettes. Blood was pouring out of his mouth and his breathing was fading. His eyes looked around at his surroundings. He could see his friend laying with no arm. He could see a woman fallen to the ground. His eyes filled with bloody tears as he saw his love laying in the fire, burning, and quiet. His vision faded on the wolf looming over him with bits of his own legs dripping down on his face like crumbs.

    The werewolf gorged its face full of leg meat and sinew. It picked pieces of flesh off its fur and slurped it down through its fangs. The moon was hanging overhead and the wolf stared longingly at the sky. Its snout was pointed high and it let out a long howl. Aroo! Its claws extended and flexed before swiping down at the stocky man's torso. Organs spilled out onto the sand and the beast continued its feast.

CHAPTER 2

Cody Walker woke to the smell of smoke. His head was pounding as he jumped off his couch to his oven. The source of the wake up call was inside. He turned it off and peeked in to see the frozen pizza burnt to a crisp. *Great, what am I going to eat now? I shouldn't have fallen asleep. Dumb shit like that is why Shannon left you.* Cody Walker was an average man. Average looks, average weight, average height, average brains. There was little special about him and even less to remember him by.

He placed the charred pizza on top of the oven and paced around his kitchen looking for something else to eat. There were few options left. Cody hadn't left his apartment since the breakup last week. And that was the first time he had left since he lost his job the week before. *I thought she was trying to cheer me up, but nope it was another firing.*

Cody slumped back on his couch with a jar of peanut butter and a packet of saltines. He ate one peanut butter covered cracker before staring at the ceiling for a half hour. Another cracker in and another thirty minutes gone. He made a mental inventory of his apartment as he looked around. *Television, refrigerator, microwave, couch, chair.* There were memories attached to all of them.

There were even new memories forming with the amount of dishes in the sink, overflowing onto the counter, and making their way into the living room, settling nicely on the coffee table in front of the couch where he had been sleeping because his bed reminded him too much of "her." Trash was beginning to follow the same route and Cody had nowhere to the put the ruined pizza even if he had wanted to throw it out.

He grabbed his laptop and opened it up to all his social media. His failed relationship and job haunted him. He'd yet to change his relationship status or update his occupation. He instead looked at the same pictures before checking the job sites. He sent out a few applications and his e-mail lit up with the "thank you for applying" notifications. His inbox was filled with those mixed with rejection e-mails from the past two weeks. They all carried the same sappy sentiments of saying "you're not good enough for us and we're sure you'll be good enough somewhere else" or "we know you need to eat and we regret to inform you that you won't find food here."

Cody closed his computer and slid down on the couch. *Why should I even bother anymore? Shannon didn't want me. No job wants me. There's no point.* He looked down at the sweatpants he'd been wearing since the breakup and the holes in his shirt he'd hadn't changed in days. His own nostrils flared at the smell his body was taking on. It getting hard to tell if his mouth or pits stunk worse. They seemed to be in competition with each other.

His eyes darted back around the apartment. On the coffee table was a small, long black jewelry box. He grabbed for it without changing position and opened it. A gold necklace stared back at him. *I should have gave it to her. She wouldn't have left if I just gave it to her.* He shook his head and lazily stuffed another cracker in his mouth. *I could still give it to her. Maybe that'll work. Maybe it'll bring her back.*

He took out his phone and sent his ex a text. *Hey. I know you said not to keep texting, but I've got something to give you. Call me and we can find a time to meet. Or you can just come over. Let me know.* He put the phone on the table and resumed looking at the necklace. Each link looked like it were made of rope. The chunky bits resembled thick braided hair when all strung together. *If she won't enjoy it then I will.* He took it out of the box and clasped it around his own neck. The coffee table began to vibrate and he could see his phone had lit up. He answered it immediately without looking. And he began to blather uncontrollably.

"Shannon, thank God you called. I've been wanting to talk to you. There's so much I need to say. First I want to say I'm sorry and I'll try to do better. I'm going to get a new job and life will be great. We're going to be fine. And I've got this necklace for you."

The caller on the other end wasn't Shannon. A masculine voice responded. One he's known for a long time.

"Cody, bud. It's Nate. Didn't my name pop up when I was calling?"

Cody breathed out in pain and exhaustion. *Dammit Nate, why are you bothering me?*

"Oh, I guess I answered too quickly."

"Hey man, I know you're having a tough time with losing your job and Shannon leaving."

"Why are you calling me then? I thought I said I wanted to be alone. I thought I made that clear."

"Because you're my friend, idiot. I'm not going to let you sink even further into a depression. You need to get out of that apartment. Talk a walk outside, meet some new girls."

"I don't need to do anything. I don't want to do anything. I only want things to go back to the way they were."

"That's not going to happen, Code. You can mope all you want, but you should at least get some fresh air while you do it. The lack of sun isn't doing you any favors."

"How do you know I'm not out right now having a blast somewhere?"

"Is that what you're doing?"

"No."

"Listen, I don't want you taking your anger or stress or sadness out on me. I didn't call to harass you. I called to invite you to Will's beach house."

"You mean his parent's beach house."

"You know what I meant. I took off work and I'm going down for a few days. I was wondering if you wanted to come. His parents won't be there. It'll be just us guys. When's the last time the three of us went down there at the same time?"

"Probably been at least ten years."

"Are you in then? It'll do you some good to smell that salty air."

Cody looked down at his necklace and the mess his apartment had become. He sat up and crumbs fell to the floor. They too were in good company with the rest of the garbage.

"I'm going to pass. I'm sorry, Nate. I don't think I'm ready yet."

"Really? Are you sure? We're talking Holborn beach, man."

"Yeah, I can't go. I'm waiting for Shannon to call me. I'm hoping she'll want to get back together. I want to make sure I'm in town for that."

"Alright well it would have been fun to have you, but if you think you're going to get back together then I wish you luck. I know Will would have loved to see you."

"I know. I'm sorry man. Tell him I said 'hi.'"

"And I'll give you a call when I get back. Maybe we can grab lunch or dinner."

"Yeah, hit me up."

They said their goodbyes and Cody hung up the phone. He ate another saltine and went to his fridge for a drink. He poured a glass of old grape juice and could hear the table vibrate again. He sprinted back to the table and grabbed his phone. He read it this time and it was Shannon. He answered as he sat back on the couch.

"Hey Shannon, how are you?"

"I'm fine Cody. What did you want?"

"I wanted to see how you were. How things are. How life is."

"You said you had something to give me. Did I leave something at your place? I thought I grabbed everything. If this is about an old video game or vinyl record then you can keep it. I don't care."

"No. It's neither of those. It's a necklace I wanted to give to you."

"I don't want it Cody. Return it and get your money back. You'll need it."

"It's a present for you. I want you to have it. I know you'll love it."

"Childish shit like this is why I left you."

"Why did you bother calling me then?"

"To tell you that I don't care what I left there and to tell you not to call or text me anymore. I'm seeing someone else Cody. I've moved on with my life. I'm not going to be held back by you."

"It's only been a week and you met someone?"

"I was seeing him before we split Cody. I'm sorry to tell you this way."

He hung up the phone without a goodbye and drank the rest of his juice. Then he picked up the phone again and waited as it rang.

"Hey Cody, is everything alright?" said Nate.

"As alright as they can be. Did you leave yet?"

"I'm on the highway right now."

"Oh. Alright. Have fun man."

"Did you change your mind about coming? I can turn around and pick you up."

"You don't have to do that for me. I don't want to be a burden or a charity case, Nate. I'll be alright."

"Nah, fuck that. I'm turning around. I'll be there in about twenty minutes."

"Are you sure it isn't a problem?"

"Not at all. Do you think you could do me a favor?"

"Sure, what is it?"

"Get a shower and brush your goddamn teeth. I'm guessing you haven't in days."

"You got me there. I'll see you soon."

They hung up and Cody jumped to his feet. *I don't know why, but I feel good. Fuck that bitch Shannon. I'm going to go have fun without her.* He tossed what clean clothes he had left into a backpack before jumping into the shower and cleaning himself up. Swim trunks, sunglasses, and sunscreen. He put on a ball cap and heard a knock at the door. He opened it up to see Nate standing there with his arms crossed. He was tall with thin legs and looked like a scarecrow after a busy shift.

"I've been waiting for ten minutes in the truck. Thought I'd come knock."

"I didn't hear you in here."

Nate glanced his friend over.

"You look like shit Code. She really did a number on you, didn't she?"

"It hasn't been easy."

The two friends embraced each other in a hug.

"Hey uh, I'm cool with people wearing whatever they want and all, still I've got to ask; what's the deal with the necklace? If you're trying to be gangsta, I've got to tell you that you're wearing the wrong style of chain. You look more like you're a mom who's ready for a night at the opera."

"It was a present for Shannon."

"I can see she really appreciated it."

"I didn't get a chance to give it to her. I guess I never will now."

"I'm sorry to hear that. You never know though. She may come around again."

Cody's eyes were aimed at his shoes.

"I don't think so. She already met someone else. She said she was with him while we were still together. She was cheating on me, Nate."

Nate cleared his throat and threw his hands into the air.

"Fuck that bitch. If it's any consolation, women who do that will continue to do that. She'll cheat on this guy with someone else before you know it."

Nate helped with Cody's bag and they headed outside. A blue pickup was in the parking lot.

"We're taking your truck? That thing has no air."

"Would you rather drive yours with no radio? Maybe we could talk about our feelings the whole ride down. Is that what you want?"

"The truck's fine."

CHAPTER 3

It had only been a two hour trip for the boys to reach the outskirts of Holborn. Cody spent most of the time with his arm out the window surfing the air. Nate spent his time changing radio stations at every opportunity.

"Your hands spend more time on the dial than on the wheel," said Cody.

"I'm a fine driver, don't worry about it," said Nate.

They crossed a small bridge and saw the big sign reading *Holborn*. The afternoon sun still provided a warm comfort to those walking around the town. And there were a lot. Men with their shirts off, women in bikinis. Everyone was in flip flops and sandals and letting the sun direct their course. Small shops littered the town and you could find any variety of food you wanted between different pizzerias. Thrift shops, Cash4Gold, a church, and the arcade rounded the town out.

"We made some good time, didn't we?" said Cody.

"We're much faster in this truck with no air than your little car," said Nate.

Nate was hanging his head out the window at a stop sign. A group of three women were walking by.

"Damn, take a look at them, Cody. That's what I'm talking about. We need to get you a rebound while we're here."

"I don't know about that."

"You being a buzz kill already? We're here to have fun. Start having fun, dammit or I'll take you back to that crypt of an apartment."

Cody took his arm out from the window and placed it in his lap.

"Hey man, I'm only joking. I know you're not ready yet," said Nate, "But you know what we are ready for?"

"What's that?"

"Gas. This truck needs some more fuel unless we want to walk the rest of the way to Will's place."

They pulled into a gas station with a convenience store attached to it. An attendant came over and began filling the tank for Nate while Cody stepped inside the store. It seemed typical for a gas station. Snacks were in short aisles and consisted of candy, pretzels, chips, and jerky. There were cold drinks; soda, energy shots, and beer too. A large man was standing at the selection of beers and Cody squeezed by him to open the fridge up. He grabbed a case of honey beer and turned to see the big man staring at him. Cody could see that he was easily 6'5" and 350 lbs. His alcoholic odor clung to him like a calf to its mother.

"There something I can help you with?"

"That's some necklace you have there. There a prom you going to tonight?" he said.

"I was thinking about it. Why are you asking? You want to take me?" said Cody.

The man puffed his chest out and grinned. His pearly whites were anything but and there were a few missing too.

"Maybe you can give it to me instead and I won't knock your lights out," he said.

"I'm afraid it's not for sale," said Cody.

"I wasn't asking."

Cody placed his beers on the floor and tucked his chin.

A fist came towards to Cody's face and his immediate reaction was to duck. It worked and he heard the big man yelp after hitting the glass instead of Cody. The glass didn't break, but he could see that the man's knuckles had split open.

"You son of a bitch. I'm going to really get you now," he said.

A short man with slicked back hair walked over from behind a display of beef jerky. He put distance between the heavy man and Cody.

"Now Gordon, take it easy. I saw the whole thing. You picked a fight this man. He didn't say a damn word to you until you opened your mouth with an insult."

"That's cause I knew this boy was trouble by seeing him," said Gordon.

"That's a load of shit and you know it. You sure did hit the bottle early today, didn't you?"

"Bonnie left me again. I can't take this shitty life anymore."

"That's no reason to take it out on this man. Now get the hell out of here. Go back home to your fish."

Gordon turned his head to throw a dirty glare before walking out the door. The short man turned to Cody and extended a hand. Cody shook it quickly, grabbed his beers and snacks then headed for the register. The short man followed behind him.

"Hey thanks for the save, but I don't appreciate a tail."

"It was no problem. Gordon tends to take his problems out on others."

"I didn't take it personally."

"I'm Henry, I run the Cash4Gold. That chain you have would fetch you a few bucks if you want to sell it."

"I'll pass, thanks."

"You know where to find me if you change your mind."

Cody grabbed his items and took them back out to the truck. He placed them in the bed and climbed in the passenger's seat to find Nate bopping his head to the latest pop song.

"Where the fuck were you man?" said Cody.

"I've been in the truck this whole time," said Nate.

"Of course I know you were in the fucking truck. And you didn't think for a minute that I was taking too long? That maybe I needed some goddamn help in there? You left me alone."

"What happened? Are you alright?"

"I'm fine thanks to some grease ball who saved me from a drunken ape."

"Why are you talking like you're from the forties?"

"There's no better way to describe the freaks that were in that store. Let's just get to Will's now."

Ten minutes later they pulled up to Will's beach house. It was a two story home that overlooked part of the ocean. People could practically jump into the water from the second floor deck. There was also a first floor deck on the front side with railing all around it. Will was standing there when Cody and Nate got out of the truck. He was a little smaller than Cody and Nate, but made up for it by taking care of himself better. All three men exchanged hugs and Will helped bring in their belongings.

"I'm sorry to hear about Shannon and your job, but I'm glad you came to visit," said Will.

"Yeah, well Nate wouldn't take 'no' for an answer," said Cody.

"Thanks for having us," said Nate jabbing Cody in the side.

The three men stepped inside and were greeted by antique furnishings. An old rifle hung on the wall in the living room, a few glass cabinets stood on the first floor, a desk sat near the stairs with a letter opener speared into a stack of papers.

There was a kitchen, a living room with a banister overhang, the master bedroom, and a bathroom on the first floor. The second floor had another bathroom and two more bedrooms.

"This place looks different from how I remember," said Cody.

"Yeah my parents decided to redecorate it. My mom got real big into antiques."

"It doesn't exactly give off a beach vibe anymore, does it?" said Cody.

"My parents got tired of the shells, starfish, and anchors everywhere."

"Surely there's a middle ground between beach vomit and haunted mansion. It looks like the set of a Hammer Horror movie. Is Christopher Lee going to pop out from behind a corner?"

"Is that the first of many references I won't understand? On a more relevant note, you can have the first room, Cody and the second's for you Nate. I'll be staying downstairs," said Will.

"Sounds good to me," said Cody.

"Now you mind if I ask you something? Why are you wearing that necklace? How are we going to get girls if you're wearing that ugly thing?" said Will.

"Why's everyone bothering me about the necklace? It was a gift for Shannon. I spent a lot of money on and it's going to get worn by someone, dammit. Even if that someone is me."

"That's a strange way to say you lost the receipt," said Will.

"You said mine's the first room right? I'm going to go check it out. You mind putting the beer away for me?" said Cody.

Cody headed up the stairs leaving Will and Nate behind.

"What's his problem?" said Will.

"I don't know. He had some sort of run in with someone while I was getting gas," said Nate.

"He's acting like someone ran over him with a car. I'm glad you're both here, but I hope he livens up a little."

Will carried the beers into the kitchen to the fridge. Nate was following in tow and checking out everything. A statue of a mallard was placed near the trash can and windows.

A cabinet full of dishes and silverware was displayed prominently near the kitchen. Forks, knives, spoons hung inside as if they were trophies to be admired. Will smiled as Nate examined them.

"That's pure silver, baby. The real deal."

"Are we going to eat with them?"

"You kidding me? My mom would kill me if we used them," said Will.

"What's the point in having utensils if you can't use them?"

"They're meant to be admired."

"Oh in that case, they're doing their job well."

Cody opened the door to his room. A long European sword hung across the bed. The bedside table had what looked like a small cauldron and a squat pull door was on one of the walls. Another wall had sliding door windows with drawn curtains. *Strange shit in here too, I see.* There were of course normal items too; a dresser with a mirror above it, a closet, and the bed itself that looked comfortable enough for two. Cody unpacked and stepped outside on the balcony. The sun was beginning to set and he inhaled the sea air. A couple of seagulls were playing in the water below and he could nearly touch them when he stretched his arms out.

He went back downstairs to find the others in the living room. Nate was sitting on the couch playing with the letter opener. It resembled a small golden dagger. He was tossing it in the air and grabbing it by the handle. Will was looking on his phone while drinking a beer. There was an unlit fireplace on the far wall with fire pokers laying near it.

"Why's there a fireplace in a beach house?"

"Its adds a cozy atmosphere and it's nice in the winter."

"But doesn't it stink?"

"No, it's propane based."

"Why's there a fire poker set by it then?"

"For at-mos-phere. The hell's the matter with you?"

"And I'm guessing that sword in my room is atmosphere too? It isn't going to fall on me in the middle of the night, is it?" said Cody.

"You mean, Aconite?"

"It has a name?"

"Apparently. That's what my dad calls it anyway. Don't worry, it's pretty secure on the wall. I wouldn't let you sleep in there if I didn't think it was safe."

Cody sat down next to Nate.

"I'm more interested in that gun," said Nate.

He had caught the letter opener again while his eyes were locked on the rifle across the room.

"That's a Pennsylvania long rifle. It's a black powder flint lock."

"Is that what they used during the Revolution?"

"It's a replica, but yes," said Will.

"Does that mean it doesn't fire?"

"No, it fires. I've shot it myself a couple of times, but it's a bitch to reload."

"You think we could shoot it while we're here?" said Cody.

"Look at Code taking interest in something that isn't self pity," said Nate, "Not that I'd be opposed to wanting to shoot it either."

"It's already getting too dark tonight, but maybe tomorrow we can. After we hit them beaches of course," said Will.

"Sounds great. I've got one more question for you though. What's up with the little door in my room?" said Cody.

"Oh man, that's the best addition they added here," said Will, "Go upstairs, open it and you'll see in a minute."

Cody followed the direction and headed back upstairs. He opened the small door and there was one of the beers he had bought sitting inside it. It was cold to the touch and already popped. He returned downstairs sipping the beer.

"Your parents put a dumb waiter in their beach house?"

"Pretty cool, right? My grand mom usually stays in that room. It's easier to bring up food for her that way."

"You put your grandma in the room with the sword?"

"She's never complained about it, unlike you."

"Enough bickering. How about we have dinner boys? I'm thinking I can make my famous pork tacos," said Nate.

CHAPTER 4

Late night was in full swing in Holborn. Midnight had just rolled by and most were still out in bars, drinking with friends, and chasing potential summer love. Gordon wasn't one of those. He was sitting in his small sea shack on a beat up armchair watching TV. He had set himself up a fine graveyard of beer around him. Bottles were everywhere and he considered it lucky for the those that didn't break. He sat with yet another beer and looked at his hand. The blood had been dry for a few hours and he didn't bother to wrap it. *I shouldn't have swung at that stupid kid.*

Gordon wasn't completely alone. There was a goldfish in a tiny bowl that was placed across the room. The two creatures would often exchange glances at each other. It was a gift from his woman before she left him. He didn't think it'd last a week, but here it was two years later. It swam in its little world consisting nothing more than the bowl and a ceramic fish house that resembled a cave. The fish was giving him the eye now.

Gordon staggered over to the bowl and bent down to be eye level with the fish.

"You miss her too, huh? Well do you think? When's that bitch coming back this time?"

The fish darted around the bowl, into its cave, and back out again.

"You don't really care who's here as long as they're giving you food. I know your game, fish."

He poured a few flakes of fish food into the bowl and it ate up. Gordon finished his beer, grabbed another and flopped back down on the armchair. He spent most nights falling asleep on the chair while watching shitty entertainment. *Bonnie had always called me to bed, but she ain't here no more.*

The movie on TV was standard fare. A woman pining for the love of a man while a monster from outer space tries to kill them both. Gordon's eyes were barely open between sips of his beer and pieces of dialogue on screen. He felt himself drifting off to sleep. A scream jolted his body back awake and he looked forward to see a man in a rubber monster suit chasing a teenager who's actress has long died. He let his head dip downward again until another noise brought him back to life. A long howl was heard right outside his window. His eyes were wide open now. He looked towards his fish and could tell it was hiding in its cave. *Must have been the damn TV again.* Onscreen was a commercial for coffee followed by another ad for pistachios.

He reached down between empty bottles to find the remote control. His hand was searching in a sea of glass and spilled beer. He managed to bring up the treasure after the third swoop. He turned off the TV and let his dreams continue. It were a good one too. A couple of beautiful women coming over just to see him and his fish. Things were about to get real nice for Gordon when another howl woke him up. He looked to the blank TV then glanced at the nearby window.

He lifted himself off the couch, took another swig from his now warm beer, and grabbed his shotgun.

"I better go take a look. Whatever it is, won't let us get any sleep anyway. You better hold down the fort while I'm gone," he said to the fish.

He checked to make sure his double barrel was loaded and he stepped outside. His shack wasn't too far from the bay. It was tucked in a bunch of grass away from the rest of the community. *Times like this makes me wish I had some neighbors.* The night air was warm and the moon helped him see his surroundings. His car was parked on the road. There was no sign of damage to it. *Nothing out of the ordinary so far. Maybe it was the wind.* He loosely held the shotgun while walking towards the water. The moonlight reflected off it providing him a decent view of the midnight bay.

There were the normal signs of life. A flock of sleeping seagulls, a couple crabs, and clams digging in the shore line.

He let out a burp and started back for his home when he fell face first into the ground. He could see something odd staring back at him as he picked himself up. Something had stuck out in the sand. Some sort of imprint. The large man craned his head to take a closer look. *I forgot a goddamn flashlight. Good going Gordon. Dumbass can't even remember to bring a light when it's dark out.* The moon allowed him to barely make out the track. There was enough light to tell that these were a set of prints unlike the other regular visitors. Each had four small indents with a larger one under it. Each smaller indent had an even smaller hole above them. Gordon stood and could see many lining the bay.

Looks like some sort of large dog print. 'Cept the way they're placed makes it look like the dog only has two paws instead of four. Must be a Great Dane practicing its circus act. Keep on at it buddy, but try to keep it down and let me get some sleep.

The heavy man laughed to himself and stumbled away from the bay.

I better call Naughton and Dunne tomorrow. Tell 'em there's a giant dog loose out here. Those fuckers would only laugh at me tonight on account of me being so damn drunk. Dammit Bon, why'd you go and leave me drinking myself to death? Get a hold of yourself Gordon. Can't let those dark thoughts seep in. Gotta stay positive. Gotta get some damn sleep while you're at it.

Gordon reached his shack within a few minutes and saw the door was wide open. *Now I know I closed that damn thing. Didn't I?* He glanced around in the night and saw no people, no cars, nothing but tall blonde grass and the sky. Gordon walked inside his home and let out a shriek.

A beast was standing by the fish bowl. It rivaled his height. No, it was taller than him. And it was bigger too. It was covered in tattered clothes and standing on two hind legs. White fur covered it and its long snout sprouted sharp teeth in every direction. He stood frozen watching the creature. Its clawed paw was inside the fish bowl. A moment later it had plucked out its prize. The goldfish was squirming in its hands. The werewolf opened its mouth and dropped the fish in. It turned its head with a snarl, locking eyes with Gordon. It had bright yellow eyes standing out against the white fluff it was surrounded by. Yellow eyes that seemed to keep Gordon in place, standing there, ready to be eaten next.

Fuck that.

He lifted his shotgun and blasted at the werewolf. But he had missed. Now the wolf was moving towards him now and he ran outside. *What the fuck was a werewolf doing in my house? What the fuck is a werewolf doing in New Jersey? I gotta get to the station. I gotta get out of here.* His feet carried his large frame as fast as they could while drunk. He found himself stumbling in the grass towards the road. His car was still parked there and he made the distance while only falling once. He held his hand on the door handle and it wouldn't budge. *I forgot my fucking keys. Goddamn it!*

Another howl rang through the night. Gordon ran from his car further down the road. He fell again and laid in the dirt. He could hear heavy breathing nearby and he looked up to see a furry figure with a bushy tail in the distance. *How'd it get out here so fast? Wait, this one's different. There's two of the fucking things?* The clothes were still tattered, but he could tell this was another werewolf. He scrambled to his feet and turned his course around. Only turning his head back to see that the other werewolf was indeed following him. He saw it howl softly and it picked up its pace gaining ground between them. The werewolf went prone, running on all fours at the large man.

He ran up the road closer back to his home. He zipped past it and was close enough to the bay to hear the breakers crashing on the beach. *Enough of this. I'm going to kill this right now. Just don't miss this time, idiot.*

He paused his running and the werewolf was right behind him. It leaped into the air with its claws extended.

Gordon held his shotgun up and blasted it again. The buckshot went right into the beast's breasts. It fell to the ground with a quiet whimper. He finally expelled his breathe. His body felt like it was ready to collapse next to the wolf. He used the shotgun as a crutch to keep himself from falling over. *Must have hit the thing's heart. Thank God.* He moved closer to the fallen wolf. Now Gordon towered over it. *Is that a dress its wearing? Did I kill some sort of she-wolf? The boys are going to get a kick out of this.* He let himself laugh and popped out the empty shells. But something was wrong. The creature beneath him started to rise. It was slow at first, its chest moving up and down again, but then the tail was twitching and its toes wiggling. The hole that he had shot was shrinking. The werewolf's wound was healing before his eyes. *Of course it's not dead, dumbass. You didn't shoot it with silver.* Gordon took off away from it and could soon hear the beast behind him again. It sounded as though the Earth itself was being torn with every step the wolf took.

He screamed in the air for help. There was no call in response. Instead he heard multiple howls. He seemed to be in the middle of them. *That could only mean they're all coming. They're all headed right for me.*

Gordon tried running, but found no more energy left in his drunken state. He held the empty shotgun as a club and his head cocked in a radius around him. The howls were moving closer. A series of yellow eyes glowed in the dark. One set to his left, another to his right, and a third directly in front of him. Three werewolves jumped out at Gordon. The one in front of him had lifted its snout at the others. They let an 'aroo' before slashing their paws at the heavy man. He swung his shotgun and was met with it being knocked out of his hands. He was pushed to the ground and both wolves were on top of him. He yelled as they ripped up his stomach with their claws. Then Gordon couldn't scream. Nothing would come out. He was choking on air, watching them slurp his guts. The third werewolf lorded over him, bending down with an open mouth and engulfing his head. Gordon's head was torn off with a crunch and swallowed whole.

The three werewolves howled at the moon in victory. They embraced each other while taking turns eating parts of their kill. There were only a few bits of Gordon when they were done. Chunks of intestine, a hand, and a couple toes that had fallen out of their mouths between bites of the foot. They ran off, satisfied with their night, and headed into the grass.

CHAPTER 5

Cody woke to the sound of someone pounding on his door. His own head was pounding from staying up late drinking and playing catch up with the guys. He looked at his phone and it read 9:25. Sun was pouring through the windows and he rolled over to avoid their light. Another set of knocks came at the door.

"Rise and shine, bitches. It's after 9 am! Come on boys, we have a long day ahead of us. Lots of fun, waves and women to catch," yelled Will from the hallway.

Cody cracked all his joints and looked out the balcony. The morning was alive with gulls flying and the water below gently smashing into the sand. He quickly got dressed and headed downstairs. Nate and Will were already sitting at the kitchen table drinking coffee. He poured himself a cup and pulled up a chair.

"How was sleeping with Aconite? I see you survived the night," said Will.

"I'm pretty sure I was so drunk that I wouldn't have noticed if it fell on my head," said Cody.

"I slept like a goddamn baby. It felt good knowing I didn't have to get up for work today. Plus this house has the craziest shit in it. I can see why your parents decided to abandon the nautical theme," said Nate.

"What are you talking about?" said Will.

Nate reached into his pocket and slammed down a hunk of metal on the table; knuckle dusters.

"Shit, I didn't know we had brass knuckles in the house," said Will.

"Your dad in the mob? He holding out on the big guns somewhere?" said Nate.

Cody grabbed and held them in a fist. He mimed a few punches and tossed them around between his hands.

"They have a nice weight to them. I could really knock that guy out who took Shannon from me," said Cody.

"We just woke up and you're already talking about your ex. What a great way to start the day. You're playing with brass knuckles, slept under a sword, and hanging with your friends. Shannon would have never gone for any of that," said Nate.

"I guess you're right. I'm sorry guys. I didn't mean to kill the mood. I'm going to try stay positive from now on. No more bringing down the good times."

"It's all good, right Nate?" said Will.

"Absolutely. I know breaking up is hard. I've had my fair share, but we're going to get you through this buddy."

Cody placed the knuckles back on the table and Nate picked them up.

"These things are cool, but I've always wanted one of those trench knives. Y'know the ones they used back in the first world war. They were half knuckles, half knife. All business," said Nate.

"I don't know what you're talking about, but I do know you don't need one of those. And please give me that."

Nate handed over the knuckle dusters and Will placed them in a cabinet drawer.

"I can't have these leaving the house. I'm pretty sure they're illegal in Jersey. I don't want any fines and I'm sure my parents don't want them confiscated."

"Everything fun is illegal in Jersey."

"Not everything buddy. There's still some secrets this state has up its sleeves."

"What do you mean by that?"

Will cracked a smile on his face as if he were holding back a secret. He took a deep sip of his coffee, placed it on the table and leaned into the others.

"How about we finish up here? And then we'll head for the beach and you can see for yourselves," said Will.

"Isn't it right out back? I can literally see it from my room," said Cody.

"That beach is okay, but I was thinking to take you to the real deal."

"The real deal? I'm not trying to play any beach game show bullshit." said Nate.

"No dammit. It's not a fucking game show. I didn't want to spoil the surprise, but fuck it. We're on vacation and I may as well tell you what you're getting into. I'm talking about a place where all the chicks go to show it off."

"Are you talking about a nude beach? I don't think that's such a good idea," said Cody.

"I thought you said you were going to try to stay positive," said Will.

"I am, but I don't want to show my dick off in public."

"Don't worry. Had you let me finish, I would have clarified that only the women get nude there. You won't have to sweat us seeing your little dick."

"You take me to a nude beach and you'll see how big my dick gets," said Cody.

"That sounded really wrong," said Nate.

"He knows what I mean."

"So you're down for it then?" said Will.

"Oh we're in," said Cody.

They finished their breakfast, packed beers, loaded up Nate's truck with some chairs and headed for the beach. Will's parents sure had picked a location to buy a house. That special beach was within a five minute drive of their place. They parked on the road and were the only vehicle there. The three men looked around and only saw houses in the distance. It was quiet beyond the seagulls and the sounds of waves. They made their way onto the beach and looked around.

Sand stretched on for what looked like miles. The sun was shining down on the water and it looked inviting. But there was one small problem. The beach was empty. No naked women. No clothed women. No women at all. No men either.

"There's no one fucking here. It's absolutely deserted. Have you actually been here before?" said Nate.

"Well no, but I had heard it's the place where the action happens," said Will.

"I think you've been had, man," said Nate.

Will took out his phone and starting searching on the net.

"I'm sure I can find the right place. This must be some sort of mistake."

"Clearly," said Nate.

Cody had already rooted himself down on a chair in the sand. His feet were loose and buried in the beach.

"Hey, I'm not complaining. I've never had a beach to myself before. I think this will be nice."

"At least he's staying positive," said Nate, "Forget about it Will. Looks like it's just us guys today."

All three sat down in their chairs, popped some beers, and played some tunes. The water was calm when Cody decided to take a dip. It was shallow, cold, and refreshing to get out of the hot sun. He was swimming for a good ten minutes when he saw three figures coming onto the beach. He went back on land and to the others. Nate was passed out with sunglasses on, a beer in hand, and headphones plugged in his ears. Will had his eyes glued to a paperback. Cody tapped Nate and cleared his throat for Will.

Both men came to their senses and Cody tossed his eyes at the newcomers to the beach. The boys could see them more clearly now. Three women had made camp within thirty yards.

The tallest of the group had brown hair and was wearing a swim skirt with a tight top. She was lounging in a beach chair and already had a book out.

The short lady sat directly on the sand. She had black hair and was wearing one piece suit.

The last woman was between their heights, but seemed to be calling the shots. The boys picked up on this immediately and bickered between themselves who called the shots out of them. This "leader" was the only one in a true bikini. Her red hair bounced off her white bathing suit and the boys argued whether her hair was dyed or not. They settled on it not mattering.

"Looks like that one's for you, Code," said Nate.

"Why's that? I thought we just decided Will was our leader. Shouldn't we match up our leaders?"

"That may be, but I know that Will has a weakness for muscle girls. And I have a weakness for shorter girls. And you will probably say something stupid to any girl. So that at least gives us a fair shot at the ones we like."

Will nodded while his eyes were locked onto the tall woman.

"She likes to read too," said Will.

"See? You already have something in common," said Nate.

"What's the plan here boys? We going over there or are we waiting to see if there's about to be a show?" said Will.

"I don't think there's any show, Will. Our best bet is to go over and talk to them. There's three of us and three of them. If they mention any boyfriends then we'll walk away," said Nate.

"Are we really going to do this?" said Cody.

"You've got to get back on the horse sometime. Think of it as practice," said Nate.

"But I'd rather not. I was enjoying the seclusion."

"Hey, we won't make you go over there with us, but it's going to look strange if you stay behind. They're going to think it's weird which will make them think that we're weird. Don't do that to us. You don't have to say a goddamn word, but it'd help for you to come over," said Will.

"Fine, we're in this together," said Cody.

"I'm digging the positivity, man," said Nate.

The women seemed oblivious to the men who were approaching them. Will cleared his throat and the redhead lowered her sunglasses. Nate was standing by his side while Cody hung behind them.

"This beach is supposed to be abandoned. You boys shouldn't be here," she said.

"Really cause we thought it was a nu-"

Nate's words were cut off by a playful poke from Will.

"What he means is we thought it was a new beach," said Will.

"You thought wrong. It's meant to be abandoned. It's meant to be my private beach. And who are you three that dared come to my private beach? What are your names?"

The men looked at each other. Nate and Will had no words. Cody stepped in front of them.

"I'm Cody Walker, that's Nate Waggner, and he's Will Whale."

"All your last names begin with 'W?'"

"Yeah we met in homeroom during middle school. Been friends ever since," said Cody.

"Unfortunately," said Nate laughing.

"Now that I have your names, I can report you to the police," she said.

The boys looked at each other again. They started to slowly turn away when they heard the red head starting to laugh. The short woman and tall woman joined in.

"I'm just kidding. I don't own this beach. I'm Brett, the tall one's Maya, and Allison is our resident dwarf," she said.

"I'm not that short," said Allison, "And at least I'm not in another time zone like Maya."

"It's better than being dependent on people to grab milk off the top shelf of the fridge," said Maya.

"Ladies, please don't bicker. We've got company," said Brett, "What do you boys want anyway?"

"We were wondering if you want to combine camps. We've got plenty of beer to share," said Cody.

"We aren't supposed to drink on the beach," said Brett.

"Ah, right. Well, uh-"

"I'm kidding again. I'm sure we'd all love a nice cold one."

Allison stared at her phone then alerted the other ladies. She whispered in Brett's ear and Brett perked up.

"I'm so sorry boys, but we've got to get going. It was real nice to meet all of you. Maybe we'll see you again soon. Maybe we can have dinner together sometime. We think it'd be nice to get to know you more," said Brett.

The three women packed their gear up and were out of sight within a minute. The boys returned to their set up and popped open a fresh round of beer.

"'Get to know you more?' They barely got to know us at all," said Nate.

"Except Cody here telling them our last names. What the hell did you do that for?" said Will.

"I don't know, they just came out. I guess old habits die hard. That's what they say, isn't it?"

"Who's saying that? I want to slap them in the goddamn face with those knuckle dusters," said Will.

"I think you handled yourself fine Code," said Nate.

CHAPTER 6

The boys had spent the rest of the afternoon relaxing on the beach. No one else had bothered to visit them. Cody had his seclusion and he was basking in it. Nate was still listening to music and Will had finished his book. He placed it on his lap and finished his drink.

"You boys about ready to head out?" he said.

Nate took off his headphones and asked Will to repeat himself.

"He asked if we wanted to head out," said Cody.

"Yeah, I'm thinking we've got enough sun. Maybe it's time for some food instead," said Will.

"Let's do it. I could go for some crabs or clams or anything that comes from the sea," said Nate.

They left the beach, packed up the truck and started on the road. It didn't take long for them to realize they had a tail. A police cruiser had been following them for a block and they didn't seem to be changing their direction.

"What the hell are they following us for? You're not speeding Nate," said Will.

"Who knows? Maybe that Brett woman really reported us."

"She was only joking, calm down. We don't even know if they're after us," said Cody.

The police lights flicked on. The boys' faces didn't try to mask their concern.

"Alright, maybe they are after us," said Cody.

"What are we going to do?" said Will.

"We're going to pull over," said Cody.

"What about all the beer in the back?" said Will.

"Don't worry, they're sealed," said Nate.

He pulled the truck off to the side of the road. The cop car followed suite.

"Play it cool guys. We don't even know what we did," said Nate, "And I don't want to hear any junior lawyer shit from you Will."

"Hey I'll keep my mouth shut as long as they don't say anything stupid."

"Let's all try to keep our mouths shut," said Cody.

Two officers got out of the cruiser. They were both dressed in uniform blues. One was bald and clean shaven. The other one took all of the first's hair. He had a mustache and a trim cut, but thick head of hair. The bald one looked a little younger than his hairier partner.

"Isn't it a little odd for there to be two cops on a traffic stop?" said Cody.

"I don't know. There were always two of them in old buddy cop movies," said Nate.

The younger bald cop was the one who approached the window. Nate has his license, registration, and proof of insurance in his hands. The cop looked at them and walked away for a moment. The older officer was looking around the bed of the truck and he then walked away too. Both cops then approached the window together. The boys could read their tags clearly now. The one with no hair was Naughton and the mustache was Dunne.

"Hey we didn't now that beach was off limits. Honest," said Nate.

"What beach?" said Naughton.

"The one we just came from."

"You mean where we saw you park at? That's not off limits," said Dunne.

"Then why was it practically abandoned?"

"How should we know? There's plenty of beach spots here. Some are bound to be more crowded than others," said Dunne.

Dunne motioned to the truck's bed with his hands.

"You boys getting an early start to drinking today?" he said.

"Hey they're all sealed back there. I know you know that too," said Will.

"Yes, but your breath tells a different story," said Dunne.

"Hey, I'm not the one driving. I can drink as much as I damn well please," said Will.

"Don't mind him, officer. But I'd like to ask you bluntly. Is there a reason why you pulled me over this afternoon? Was I speeding? I'm pretty certain that I wasn't. I wasn't on my phone either," said Nate.

The officers shifted their heads to get a closer look at the truck's interior. They could see that three men were wedged in the truck with little room to hide anything or sit comfortably.

"It's a routine traffic stop. We only have a few questions for you before we let you go," said Dunne.

"Questions about what?" said Nate.

"The standard stuff. For starters; How long have you been in Holborn?" said Naughton.

"What's it to you?" said Cody.

"We got in yesterday," said Nate.

The two cops whispered to each other.

"What are you doing here in town?" said Dunne.

"It's summer. It's a beach town. What the fuck do you think we're doing?" said Will, "We're staying in my parent's beach house for a couple days while we're here."

"And where's that at?" said Naughton.

"I don't have to tell you that."

"No, I suppose you don't," said Dunne, "But would you mind telling us how long you three plan to stay in our town?"

The boys looked at each other and had a whisper of their own.

"For the foreseeable future," said Nate.

"That's good to hear. We might have more questions. It's comforting to know you'll be around to answer them," said Dunne.

"You haven't asked us anything worth a damn," said Will.

The officers nodded at each other.

"There's a local man in town named Gordon. Do you know him?" said Dunne.

Nate and Will shook their heads no.

"And what about you?" said Naughton.

"Yeah, I had he pleasure of meeting him yesterday when we first got to town," said Cody, "We didn't exactly hit it off."

"So we've heard. We went to the gas station and ran this truck's plates off the security footage," said Dunne.

"Why would you bother doing that? Did something happen to him?" said Cody.

"Why would you care?" said Naughton.

"I suppose I don't. But I do care that you're eating up our valuable vacation time. I don't exactly get out often and I'd like to enjoy this sunlight while it lasts."

"He's gone missing is what happened," said Dunne.

"In a day? You're telling me someone hasn't been seen since yesterday afternoon and you're out here running plates and pulling people over?" said Will.

"Gordon isn't the type of guy who'd up and leave without telling anyone. Hell, his whole life has been a vacation. He's got nowhere to go," said Dunne.

"I'm starting to see why you pulled us over. You think I had something to do with his disappearance? Shouldn't I have a lawyer for this type of shit?"

"Hey now, we're not saying anything of the sort. This is a routine traffic stop, remember? We're merely asking you some additional questions," said Dunne.

"Yeah like why is it that you're wearing a woman's necklace, Mr.-" said Naughton.

"Walker."

"Yes. Mr. Walker, do you always wear such items?" said Naughton.

Cody held up the necklace and chomped down on it.

"It sure is pretty isn't? Tastes good too."

"You wear it because it tastes good?"

"I wear it because I can wear whatever I want without having to explain it to police."

"But that's what your argument with Gordon was about, wasn't it?"

Will put his arm across Cody as if to hold him back from moving. Not that Cody had budged or even the space to twitch.

"You don't have to answer that Cody," said Will.

"I'm only asking him a simple question," said Naughton.

"I don't think this Gordon guy is missing at all. I think they know exactly where he is," said Will.

"What the fuck are you talking about?" said Dunne, "We have no idea where he is. We wouldn't be here if we did."

"Yes you do. I have a feeling he's dead. I'm basing that off the fact that you're talking to my friend like a goddamn murder suspect."

"Is that what's going on here? You think I killed him? You think I came into town and killed a guy during my first night of vacation? Are you out of your fucking mind?" said Cody.

"Well, did you?" said Naughton.

"Of course I didn't kill him. He made fun of my necklace, but I wouldn't kill someone over that. It's a woman's necklace. I know that. And you saw the footage. He swung at me first. I didn't even raise a fist."

The two cops did their whisper trick again, stepping away from the truck and huddling together.

"We'll be honest with you. We don't think you kill him."

"But he is dead?"

The officers held their heads.

"Yes, but you're not a suspect. We're only checking in to see if you've seen anything weird or had any strange encounters," said Naughton.

"You mean aside from this?"

"We did see something," said Nate.

The officers perked up and Dunne had a notepad out.

"Yes? Go on," he said.

"Yeah, we were on the beach back there and turns out we vacation at the same place as the Loch Ness monster. We caught Nessie getting her tan on," said Nate.

Dunne put his notepad away.

"If you're going to waste our time then I think we're done here."

"Oh so it's okay for you to pull us over to waste our time. Then you make my friend think he's accused of murder, but a joke on you is too far? I see how it is," said Nate.

"We're only looking out for the people of Holborn. It's a busy season. We appreciate your understanding."

"We don't understand shit," said Nate.

"That's for the best then," said Naughton.

"You boys have a good day, enjoy your time in our lovely town, and try to stay out of trouble," said Dunne.

The officers began walking away from the truck. Naughton had climbed into the passenger's seat and Dunne nearly got into the driver's when Nate yelled out the window to them.

"Hey wait, what about all my shit?" said Nate.

Dunne bent down into his cruiser and popped out a second later. The cop returned to the truck and handed Nate his information. On top was a gray business card. It Dunne's first name, number, and an e-mail address.

"What's this for?" said Nate.

"In case you need to get in touch with us," said Dunne.

"How thoughtful," said Nate slipping the card into his wallet.

The cops got back into their car and the boys were alone again. They pulled away in their cruiser and the truck started up. Nate pulled it back onto the road and they were off. The police car was already long out of view.

"That was weird, wasn't it?" said Cody.

"Absolutely," said Will, "I can't believe they treated you like that Cody."

"Hey, it's alright. You don't think they think I'm really a suspect do you?"

"They said they didn't think you killed him," said Nate.

"Yeah, but they could be lying. It wouldn't be the first time a cop ever lied to someone."

"That's true."

"They might be trying to build a case against you."

"I don't know. I think there's something else going on that they didn't want to tell us."

Nate had been driving the truck around the block as they talked. He had circled past where they were pulled over.

"Now what do we do? Where am I driving to?" said Nate.

"You two still want to get something to eat?" said Will.

"Absolutely. I better enjoy a nice warm meal while I still have the chance. They might try to lock me up next time they see me," said Cody.

"Alright, I know a great diner that's BYOB," said Will, "We can grab some food and still shoot the rifle if we get back to the house in time."

CHAPTER 7

The men pulled up to the diner. It was a typical Jersey establishment. Cars were packed in the lot and you could see that it was the same inside with people. The trio could see the waitresses scuttling around booths, delivering food, and taking orders.

"Looks like we're in for a long wait," said Nate.

"Then we better get in before anyone else does," said Will.

Nate and Will headed for the front door. Cody took his time, falling behind, but yelled ahead for their attention. His two friends turned back with a 'what' tilt to their heads. Cody gave a tilt of his own to a group of women who were walking up to the diner. Not just any group of women. The same three women who they had met on the beach.

They weren't in their beach clothes any longer. The short one, Allison was in shorter shorts. The tall one, Maya was in tight black jeans. And their leader, Brett was wearing a blue summer dress. The men were practically panting over the sight of them. They had to pick up their jaws like a wolf in a Tex Avery cartoon.

"Shouldn't we go over there and talk to them?" said Cody.

"We absolutely should and we absolutely are going to," said Will.

"Look at you Code, taking action. I'm liking this single life version of you," said Nate.

The men walked over and all three let out a whistle. The women turned their heads and laughed.

"If this isn't a coincidence then I don't know what is," said Cody.

"Oh hey girls look, it's the beach boys. First you go to our exclusive sunbathing spot and now you're at our favorite diner. Are you boys stalking us?" said Brett.

The men through their hands in their air.

"You caught us," said Nate.

"Looks like we're done for," said Will.

"We better get out of here while we can," said Cody.

"On the contrary, you better stick around," said Brett.

"It'd be a shame for you three to run out on us," said Allison.

"Like what you did to us earlier?" said Nate.

"We had something to do, but now we've got all the time in the world," said Maya.

"You all got changed fast," said Will.

"It's been hours since we've seen each other," said Maya.

"Oh, right."

"Yeah, I guess you can tell we haven't been back to our house yet. We got a little held up by the police," said Nate.

"The police? What for? Did they give you a ticket for speeding on vacation?" said Allison.

"They think Cody here killed someone."

"I see we're dealing with a dangerous man," said Brett, "Be careful ladies."

"You didn't do it, right?" said Allison.

"Of course not," said Cody, "It's all some sort of misunderstanding I'm sure."

"Yeah Cody here wouldn't hurt a fly," said Will.

"Let's hope not," said Brett.

"It looks packed in there. Maybe we should we try to get a table together?" said Cody.

"Why not? I know you boys would try to sit near us anyway. There's no getting away from you," said Brett.

"Alright, I'll go in and see how long the wait is," said Nate.

Nate headed in while the women tracked his every step.

"So you ladies walked here?" said Cody.

"You saw us walking didn't you?" said Brett.

"Hey, you never know, you could have parked down the street."

"We walked here. We walk everywhere," said Allison.

"It's good for the toes," said Maya.

"And the weather's so nice that we can't resist it," said Brett.

Nate returned to the group with a scowl.

"It seems like we're going to be waiting at least an hour," he said.

"We could make our own dinner in that amount of time and for half the cost," said Will.

"That's a great idea," said Allison.

"What is?"

"You making us dinner. How do you like the sound of that?"

"It sounds better than waiting around here," said Maya.

"What do you boys think? Should we eat at your place instead? Or do you enjoy waiting around?" said Brett.

"I think we're all in agreement to go back to my house, right guys?" said Will.

"As long as they don't mind riding in the back," said Nate.

"We don't mind, do we girls?" said Brett.

They all shook their heads no enthusiastically.

"We better be quick unless you want the cops to pull you over twice in one day," said Allison.

The women climbed into the bed of the truck and Nate pulled out of the lot. They bounced in the back as the boys crammed into the front.

"Is this a good idea? I know it seems fun in the heat of the moment, but think about it. We barely know these people," said Cody.

"Don't be getting negative on us again. You were the one who wanted to approach them in the parking lot," said Will.

"Yeah because I thought we could grab a booth together. Not invite them back to your parent's beach house. What do you think Nate?"

"I think it's too late to change our minds now. We'll go with it and see what happens," said Nate.

55

They pulled up to the house and everyone hopped out of the truck. The sun was already beginning to set when they walked in.

"Nice place you got here, Will," said Maya

"Thanks, it's not a bad place to stay," he said.

"Not bad at all," said Allison, "And look at all this weird shit. It's a nice change from the nautical theme."

The women admired the antiques while the men cooked up a quick dinner. They used some of the leftover pork taco supplies to make a gravy for pasta.

"Mmm, I love a good meat sauce," said Allison.

"You mean meat gravy," said Brett.

"We're not doing this here in front of the guys," said Maya.

"Oh no, I think we are," said Nate, "And she's right. It's sauce, not gravy."

"It's gravy, you uncultured asshole," said Cody.

"See you what you did?" said Maya to Allison.

"I think we can all agree that it doesn't matter," said Will.

"Typical Will, always trying to mediate," said Nate.

The men changed their clothes and came back to see the table was set. The women had used the silverware from the cabinet. Will's eyes were wide upon seeing them there, but Nate reassured him it'd be okay. *They looked better on that table than stored away untouched.* All of them took their places at the table. They paired off the way they had planned it. Will sat with Maya, Nate with Allison, and Cody with

Brett. They began eating immediately out of hunger and paused a few minutes in to realize no one was talking.

"Guess it means its good, right?" said Brett.

"What does?" said Cody.

"All the silence," she said, "But I'm breaking it. And I'm breaking it with cliches. It's time for your interview boys."

"Let us have it," said Nate.

"Well what do you boys do for starters?" said Brett.

"Should we speak for each other or do you want us to answer one on one?" said Cody.

"I guess I'll start. I'm an engineer," said Nate, "Pays well too. Some of the perks include a couple weeks vacation that increase with every year worked."

"I like a hands on man," said Allison.

"What about you Will?" said Maya.

Will paused shoving his face full of penne. He wiped his mouth and took a sip of beer.

"I'm starting law school in the fall," he said.

"I like the sound of that," said Maya.

"That's good to hear. My main motivator is impressing women."

"And you Cody?" said Brett.

"Yes? What about me?"

"What do you do for a living?"

"I'm a little in between jobs, let's say. At the fork in the road of career opportunities."

"You're unemployed then?"

"To put it bluntly, yes."

"I always get stuck with the slackers, don't I girls?" said Brett.

The women let out a howl of laughter. Cody looked to his men for comfort and found none.

"Don't be so hard on yourself. I'm sure something will come along," said Brett.

He took another plate full of pasta and a long sip of his beer, holding it in agreement.

"And what do you women do?" said Nate.

"Oh us? We're bitches," said Brett laughing, "Full time."

"Come on now, Brett. That's only our hobby," said Allison.

"They sure love their jokes, don't they? I'm a life coach," said Maya.

"You mean telling people how to exercise? Getting people's lives together? That sort of thing?" said Will.

"All of that and more," said Maya, "Some people appreciate a guiding hand when they're lost in life."

"How about you Allison?" said Nate.

"I'm in real estate," said Allison.

"Oh yeah, how are you liking that?" said Nate.

"It's not bad. People are always going to need somewhere to live. I like being the one to help them find their homes."

"And what about you Brett?" said Cody.

She stretched out her arms and a giggle came over her. It started out small, but erupted into a full blown cackle.

"I'm next to you at the fork in the road," she said, "But it looks more like a spoon to me."

"It's nice to know I'm in good company," said Cody.

She placed her hand on his knee and held it firmly.

"You have no idea," she said.

Cody's pocket vibrated loudly. Brett could feel it through his shorts. She took her hand off his leg with another laugh. The others looked at him and he took out his phone. It was Shannon calling. Nate and Will tossed him a dirty look. Cody stood with the phone in his hands.

"Excuse me ladies, I have a phone call."

The boys shook their heads at him while he went outside to answer it.

"How am I meant to go on with my life if you call me up like this? You wanted me to move on and I am."

"That's a hell of a way to answer the phone, Cody. I see a lot has changed since yesterday when you texted begging to see me."

"I wasn't begging, Shannon. I had a present for you is all."

"How about we get together tonight and you give it to me?"

"I'm guessing things didn't work out with that other guy."

"You really know how to kill a mood, don't you Cody? I'm doing my best to be nice and you're only trying to hurt me."

Cody looked up at the night sky. You could see all the stars out here. It wasn't like the bigger Jersey towns. The moon was big and bright to match his new found confidence. The sea air felt good too. It lifted his spirit, filled him with strength and a sense of purpose.

"Shannon, even if I wanted to, I couldn't see you tonight."

"Of course you could, baby. I don't care if your place isn't cleaned up."

"It's not that. I'm not at home. I'm in Holborn with Nate and Will."

"You have no job and you're having fun at the beach?"

"I met someone too. I'm not saying anything is going to happen, but I'm not going to do this 'getting back together shit over the phone' so I feel guilty and don't try to make a move. I'm going to enjoy my stay here and maybe we can talk when I get back."

"You're a real asshole, Cody."

"Have a good night Shannon. I hope you enjoy being alone."

Cody hung up and headed back inside. He greeted the others with a smile on his face. They were still gathered around the table. Cody had heard their laughter from outside. The atmosphere around the table was happy, lighthearted, jovial. It was a mood he hadn't felt in a long time. He took his seat and Nate whispered to him.

"Everything alright?" said Nate.

"It is now. What'd I miss?"

"Not too much. We were discussing what we should have for dessert," said Will.

"And what did we decide on?" said Cody.

He could see the smile on the women's faces.

"We were thinking we take our desserts to the bedroom," said Brett.

CHAPTER 8

The men and women had retired to their respective rooms. They had all made love in a wondrous fashion and the clock read five minutes to midnight when Cody checked his phone. He admired the woman who was laying in his bed. Or rather his friend's parent's beach house guest bed that he was currently sleeping in. Brett's short red hair popped against her body and she smiled when she noticed him staring at her. She sat up in the bed and he laid his head in her lap. The golden ropes hung down from his chest and she playfully stuck her face in them.

"I've been meaning to tell you that I love this necklace," she said.

"Oh? Really? It's not really mine," he said taking a moment to think it over, "Well I guess it is now. I'll be sure to keep wearing it if you like it."

"I like a man who isn't afraid to be feminine. You pull it off so well Cody."

Nate was laying with his arms above his head in pure bliss. Allison was between his legs and he enjoyed every moment. She finished up and she nestled up beside him.

Nate looked over the short beautiful woman that clung to him. Her soft body was a joy to touch. Her skin was warm, smooth and comforting. Her long black hair draped over her breasts. He moved it aside and a long scar stared back at him.

"Something you don't want to talk about?" he said.

"Not on the first night," she said.

"I understand. I'm sorry if even asking is awkward for you."

"It wasn't, but now it is."

"My most sincere apologies, little lady."

"You're a weirdo, Nate, but I like it."

"And how can this weirdo make it up to you?"

"Oh I think you'll find a way."

Allison shifted her body on top of Nate and kissed him. Her hands explored down below and Nate's eyes opened wide.

Will came out from between Maya's legs. He kissed every inch of her over until he reached her lips. Every piece of her looked sculpted. She was tough and lean and had proven it during their love making.

"How did you get such a body?" said Will.

"It's the result of hard work, discipline, and dedication," said Maya, "You could have it too if you tried."

"What's wrong with my body?"

"Nothing, but if you want muscles, you've got to earn them."

Will flexed his bicep and motioned for her to squeeze it. She did and let out a laugh.

"Not bad for someone who doesn't work out."

"But I do work out."

"Then you better start taking it more seriously. I'll have to set you up with a better routine."

"You'd do that?"

"I could always use another work out partner, but how about you get back to work down there first?"

Will dove back down between her legs. He kissed her thigh and felt rough skin. There was a half foot scar running down there. *I wonder what caused this? Looks like someone took a knife to her. Maybe that's why she stays so fit now. Or maybe she just likes working out. Don't question things so much. Enjoy what you have in front of you.*

Brett sunk down and laid her head on Cody's chest. It felt good. He felt good. He could see her whole body lit by the moon light leaking through the window. Brett looked up at Cody with her eyes turning a shade of yellow. *Wait a minute? Yellow eyes? They weren't yellow a minute ago.* Brett's body began to shake on top of Cody. And not in a pleasurable way. He gently pushed her off him and hopped off the bed.

"What's wrong with you? Are you feeling okay?"

She had no response. Her yellow eyes locked with his as her head began to split open. It was as if someone were tearing her skin off like an orange peel. Chunks of flesh covered the bed. Cody had expected to see blood underneath, but there was little to be seen. Instead her skin was being replaced with fur. Then he let himself scream.

Nate was half asleep when he heard his friend yell. He looked to his side and saw a wolf's head on Allison's small body looking back at him. She was bent in a crouching position. Her spine was popping out of her still human back. Spikes rose out of her and fur was falling down from them, covering her torso. He too couldn't hold back a scream.

Will was already awake watching Maya change before his eyes. Her head had sprung wolf ears, a long snout, and snarling teeth. Her torso had become covered in white hair. Her powerful hands turned into powerful paws with claws at the end of each finger. Her strong thick legs burst into fur clad hindquarters. A snow white fluffy tail sprung out from above her sculpted bottom. Will had heard his friends scream and he tried, but couldn't get a peep out.

Cody slowly backed towards to the bedroom door as the Brett-wolf was busy eating her former skin. Her paws were stuffing pieces of herself back into her long mouth and swallowing them without any chewing. He opened the door while still keeping a watch on the beast in his bed. He stepped into the hallway and slammed the room shut. He ran downstairs and found Will already there shaking in the living room. He was standing by the fireplace, clutching a poker in his hands. The two stood there and barely moved.

"What the fuck is going on? Where's Nate?" said Cody.

"They're fucking werewolves, man. You brought werewolves into my parent's house. How the fuck am I going to explain this?" said Will.

"We'll be lucky to explain this if we can. Now where's Nate?"

The sound of stampeding feet raddled the house. They were only a few foot steps then a yipe as Cody and Will saw Nate jump over the railing onto the couch near them. Nate hopped off the couch and joined them in their standing huddle.

"Holy shit, are you alright?" said Cody.

"No, I'm not alright. Allison torn off her goddamn skin and started to eat it."

"We know. They're werewolves," said Will.

"What are we going to do?" said Nate.

"No wonder they wanted to fuck us," said Will.

"I imagine they're no longer interested in fucking us. I think they're looking to eat us," said Cody.

"They had to go and ruin a perfectly good night. Allison was way hairier than I'm used to too," said Nate.

"They're all hairier now, Nate," said Cody.

The boys could hear the howls start up in the house. The first rang out from Cody's room. The second came from Nate's. The third from Will's. The could hear doors opening and more footsteps. Nate ran over to the hanging black powder rifle, grabbed it off the wall and held it in his hands. Three sets of yellow eyes appeared around them.

"We've got to shoot them," said Nate.

"That gun takes five minutes to load. I don't even know where the powder and balls are," said Will.

"That's just great. You want us to simply offer ourselves up as dinner then?" said Nate.

Cody's eyes lit up and he smacked Nate's back.

"Did you say dinner? Alright I have an idea. They're werewolves aren't they?" said Cody.

"Yeah, I mean I don't know what you'd call them, but the look like werewolves to me," said Will.

"I'm agreeing with you, asshole. Now think about it. We used your mom's genuine silverware last night for dinner. And we didn't bother cleaning up either."

"I figured we'd clean up this morning together," said Will.

"I understand where he's going," said Nate.

"Then we better hurry up."

Nate put back the rifle and Will dropped the poker by the fireplace. The men ran to the kitchen with the eyes slowly following them. The wolves moved without making a sound. The dirty dishes were where they had left them. Plates with butter knives and forks with pieces of gravy still on them. They each picked up a knife and a fork. They held them high and crouched their bodies low. They were under the table, waiting for their prey to appear.

"What's the plan here? We're going to stab them to death with utensils?" said Will.

"If you have something better then I'm all ears," said Cody.

"It's going to work. It has to work," said Nate.

The yellow eyes were upon them now. A furry paw flicked on the lights and the wolves sniffed the air. The men were able to sneak a better look at them. They were all covered in white and their wolf forms had followed their own human body types. The Maya-wolf was the tallest at around seven feet. Brett-wolf stood at 6 and a half. The Allison-wolf was the smallest at 6 ft. All heights being massive for a wolf on hind legs trying to eat you. They look like they had been abusing roids for months and had the anger to prove it.

The boys held their breath. They huddled with their pieces of silver and clung to them. The wolves moved around the kitchen. Their claws tore apart the cabinets, ripped upon the fridge, flinging its contents everywhere. Chairs were knocked over and broken. But as soon as it started, it was over. First the Brett-wolf left the kitchen. The Maya-wolf followed. The Allison-wolf looked around and headed towards the living room. That's when Nate sneezed. He turned to his friends with tears in his eyes. *I'm so sorry,* he mouthed quietly to the others.

A clawed paw plunged under the table at Nate. Cody stabbed his fork into the wolf's forearm in return. It pulled back, carrying Nate along with it. Will and Cody slid out from under the table and jumped to their feet. The Allison-wolf held Nate in a headlock with the fork sticking out of its arm.

"Why didn't it work?" said Will, "You think that salesman ripped my mom off?"

"I don't know. Maybe I needed to stab its heart," said Cody.

"That's vampires."

The werewolf's free arm pulled the fork out and flung it on the floor. The Allison-wolf snarled at the boys. It could have been taken for laughter if it were a human. But it wasn't. She was a goddamn creature from a nightmare. And she had Nate in her grasps.

Cody charged the wolf with his knife and thrust it into the wolf's arm again. He slid between its legs and ran towards the stair case. He heard Will yell at him from the kitchen.

"What the fuck are you doing Cody?"

The desk was sitting in intact by the stairs. On top was the letter opener they had played with yesterday. Cody snatched it and headed back. His short trip away from the kitchen had alerted the other wolves and he returned with yellow eyes following him. The Allison-wolf still had Nate in her grasps. Her head turned to Cody and he gored the gold letter opener into her. It slipped in like it were cutting warm butter.

The wolf let out a horrid squeal. Her long mouth howled and she dropped Nate. He ran for cover behind the table. Cody was left standing between three wolves. The Allison-wolf continued to howl in pain. Its free paw ripped out the letter opener and it fell to the floor, covered in blood. The other two wolves looked at Cody then to each other. He could see the drool drizzling down from their snouts. Their claws were ready to lacerate him at any second. But they didn't move. They each let out a short 'roo' and fled the scene. The boys could hear them howling in the distance after they left the beach house.

Cody ran to Nate and hugged him. Will joined in. They picked up a few chairs and slumped down in them, shaking with exhaustion and fear.

CHAPTER 9

Sun shining through the kitchen window brought the men back to life. They hadn't moved since their encounter with the werewolves. They sat in their chair for hours without saying a word. One would fall asleep and the others would watch. Then they'd swap and take turns getting rest. They did this without talking. That is until that morning light returned.

Cody stood first. He helped Nate and Will to their feet.

"Are we going to talk about what happened or what?" said Cody.

"What the fuck is there to say? That we took home some women who turned out to be werewolves who wanted to eat us?" said Will.

"That about sums it nicely. You mind if I use that? It's a perfect back cover blurb for my autobiography when we get the hell out of here. Only we are stupid enough to bring home a bunch of werewolves," said Nate.

"Would you have preferred vampires? I know you always liked those goth girls back in school," said Cody.

"No. What I'd prefer is a woman who doesn't want to kill me before at least getting to know me."

"I don't know how you can keep joking right now," said Will.

"Considering it was me who was in the grips of werewolf, I think I can joke about anything I want."

They fixed some breakfast. Eggs, lots of coffee, and bacon were had while they cleaned up the kitchen. It took a few hours until everything seemed back in place. Everything that wasn't broken that is.

"What should we do? Do we go to the cops?" said Cody.

"No, I don't think that'd be a good idea," said Nate, "Our best move would be to get the hell out of here."

"What about those two who gave us their number?"

"And tell them what? That a bunch of hot chicks we picked up from the beach turned into werewolves who tried to kill us? They'll either throw us in jail or in a mental asylum."

"Or both."

"Or both!"

"No cops, Cody," said Will.

They were on their third cup of coffee each before noon. Their shakes of fear were replaced by caffeine quakes while their minds raced to match the pace.

"What do you propose we do then?" said Cody.

"Well I don't know about you or Will, but I'm thinking we kill them," said Nate.

"I thought you wanted to flee town?"

"Only after we rid it of this menace. We can't leave knowing werewolves are preying on the good and not so good men of Holborn," said Nate.

"Alright if you're serious then I'm in," said Cody, "I'm not letting two women in a row try to ruin my life without me doing something about it."

"That's a bit of a strange reason, but welcome aboard. What about you Will? We sort of need you to be in it considering this is your parent's place. We're going to have to use this as a headquarters of sorts."

Will looked to his friends. Cody wore a reluctant smile while Nate's grin was genuine. Nate had his hand outstretched on the table. Will grabbed hold and nodded.

"I'm in. Let's kill every last one of these abominations," said Will.

"Now that we're all 'in', what's the plan? What do we know about these werewolves?" said Nate.

"I know it was midnight when they changed," said Cody.

"So they always change at midnight?" said Will.

"Who knows? I doubt they obey time, but that was the time when it happened last night. I know because I checked my phone a few minutes before she went all harakiri," said Cody.

"I thought harakiri is suicide," said Will.

"What would you call tearing off your own skin then eating it?"

"He makes a good point," said Nate.

"You think they eat their skin so they're able to become human again later?" said Cody.

"Maybe they can change their form depending on who they eat," said Will.

"Don't be ridiculous. That's absolutely insane."

"And discussing how to kill a bunch of werewolves isn't?" said Nate.

"Okay, Nate's right, let's think this through. They are a bunch of were bitches, right? What were their weaknesses? How are we going to kill them? Silver didn't do a damn thing," said Will.

Nate was playing with the letter opener once more. He was flipping and catching it in his hands. He caught its hilt and held it up to the others. Blood was still visible on its short blade.

"They could have torn us all apart, but they didn't. They were afraid when Cody stabbed Allison. Silver didn't draw any blood, but the letter opener did," said Nate.

"You mean their weakness is gold?" said Will.

"Yes and if they bleed," said Nate.

"We can kill them," said Cody.

Nate plunged the letter opener into a stack of napkins on the table. Will's eyes went wide.

"What's that? What am I missing?" said Will.

"It's from Predator," said Nate.

"Oh. It's been a long time since I've seen it. Hey Cody, what made you think to use the letter opener anyway?" said Will.

"Because I saw that silver wouldn't hurt her. She didn't even flinch when I stabbed her with the knife and fork. I figured if silver doesn't work then maybe gold would," said Cody.

"Damn, man, you're a goddamn genius," said Nate.

"It's half that and half I was so scared I needed to find something to slice that bitch with."

"We're lucky it worked out in our favor then," said Will.

"Alright boys. This means we're going to need a hell of a lot more gold if we're going to kill these things," said Nate, "I'm talking gold bullets for that gun. Gold everything. What do you have here that we can melt down?"

"There's bound to be some gold around here. I'd say we shouldn't use it, but I think my parents are already going to be pissed so we may as well keep going," said Will.

"Great. No time to lose," said Nate.

The boys searched the rooms of the house. They returned to the kitchen a few minutes later with their loot. Cody had a golden serving tray. Will had a couple of rings. Nate had a pocket watch and cufflinks.

"We're going to need more than this," said Nate.

Nate and Will stared at Cody. He was still wearing the thick golden necklace around his neck.

"We could really use your necklace, Code," said Nate.

"We're not using my necklace. I still might give it to Shannon."

"I thought you were in this because you were tired of women like her ruining your life," said Will.

"Okay, but at least she never tried to eat me or my friends. She wanted to get back together last night and-"

"Don't tell me you're considering it," said Nate.

"I'm not, not considering it."

"God dammit, Cody. Fine. Keep your damn necklace and we'll just be eaten by these werewolves," said Will.

"What if we go to the Cash4Gold place? They've got to have gold there we can buy."

"I'm pretty sure they only buy gold, not sell it," said Nate.

"It's worth trying isn't it?" said Cody.

"You two go ahead. I'm going to finish cleaning up here and find some shit I think can help," said Will.

"Do you think we should splitting up like this? I'm not sure that's a good idea," said Cody.

"Relax, Code. It's the middle of the day," said Nate.

"Okay, but if something happens then it's not on me," said Cody.

They didn't know exactly where the shop was, but a half hour riding around in the truck brought them to it.

"I knew we passed it coming in," said Cody.

"Yeah, yeah," said Nate.

They headed inside. Bright lights greeted them throughout the shop and there wasn't a dark spot in the whole place. In the back sat a short man with slicked back hair behind a counter.

"That's him alright," said Cody, "I think he said his name was Henry."

The man lit up behind the counter.

"I see you've changed your mind and decided to sell that necklace of yours. I'm very glad to see you here," he said.

"We're not here to sell anything. We were hoping to buy some gold instead," said Cody.

"You boys are confused. I do not sell gold. I buy gold. For cash."

"But we need gold. Surely you have some you can sell that you haven't sent off to be melted down yet."

The short man scratched his head, shaking it slightly.

"Why do you need gold? Did you fall in love with a girl and plan to propose?"

"Why would I need gold to propose?"

"I don't know, you tell me. You're the one who needs the gold."

"Who cares what we need it for? We might need it to kill werewolves for all you know."

"I know more than you then. Cause you'll need silver for killing werewolves."

"Not these ones."

"Okay, okay. Don't tell me the reason, but okay, I'll sell you some gold."

"Fantastic. What do you have?"

The little man bent down, disappearing completely. He popped back up with a box of rings and necklaces. He laid them on the counter and let the boys take a good look. It certainly was gold.

"Three rings, two necklaces. I'll give you a friendly discount. How about nine hundred dollars."

"Nine hundred? We can't afford that," said Cody.

"It's the best I can do. It's the best deal in town," said Henry.

"It's the only deal in town," said Nate.

"Go check other towns then come back. You'll see," said Henry.

"Yeah, yeah. We'll see. Thanks a lot for nothing, Henry," said Cody.

"Please come back if you want to sell that necklace," he said.

The men walked out and bumped into their favorite cops; Naughton and Dunne. They were walking down the street and couldn't help, but make eye contact before reaching their truck.

"Staying out of trouble, boys?" said Dunne.

"We're doing our best," said Cody.

"Weren't there three of you? Where's the other one?" said Naughton, "Is he alright?"

"He's back home. He lets us go out without him sometimes. But only if we're really good," said Nate.

"We meant no offense boys, enjoy your day," said Dunne.

"Remember to let us know if you see anything strange," said Naughton.

The cops headed off down the street away from them. Nate and Cody hopped into the truck.

"Should we have told them?" said Cody.

"I thought we agreed earlier, no cops," said Nate.

Cody and Nate returned to the house empty handed.

"I'm in the kitchen," said Will, "You made it back right in time for the show."

"What happened in here?" said Nate.

The kitchen had turned into a makeshift blacksmith's den. A crucible was heating up, a bucket of water sat on the table, and pieces of paper, metal instruments, and gold were everywhere. Tall candles were in a holder in the center of the table. Nate picked up one of the metal contraptions. It had a long handle with a little scoop at the end of it.

"This is a bullet mold. This is how they did it in the old days," said Will.

"Why do you have all this shit?" said Cody.

"Most people who have black powder rifles get into the craft of making their own bullets. Plus my mom didn't want my dad keeping it at their house so that's why it's here. The gun's here for that reason too. Hell most of these decorations are the ones my parents got tired of seeing at home. How much gold did you find?"

"It was a complete waste of time," said Cody.

"Yeah, bad news is that we found none," said Nate.

"And the good news?" said Will.

"Oh, there's no good news. I don't know why I worded it that way," said Nate.

"We'll have to use what we have then," said Will.

"We did run into those cops again," said Nate, "They were real close to arresting Cody for murder."

"What, really?" said Will.

"No, but really did see them," said Nate.

"Alright, can we just get to work?" said Cody.

The gold items melted down and Will scooped the hot metal with the bullet mold. He squeezed it, revealing a small ball before letting the bucket cool it down.

"I may as well go over some tips about shooting this gun," said Will.

"What's there to know? Point and shoot," said Nate.

"Except you're forgetting about how inaccurate these rifles were along with misfiring and hang fires."

"What's a hang fire?" said Cody.

"Sometimes the gun will shoot and the bullet won't come out for up to a minute. It's somewhat rare, but it does happen and it might scare you if you don't know what's going on," said Will, "Hell this gun might scare you even when it works right. Most people flinch the first time shooting it."

"It's an old ass rifle. I'm not going to flinch from shooting it," said Nate.

"I still flinch sometimes," said Will.

"You better not. We barely have the ammo to spare."

"Speaking of, how many bullets do we have?" said Cody.

"We have six. That gives us two chances per wolf," said Will.

Six golden bullets were on the table. Will rolled paper into a short tube, closing one end and filling the other with gunpowder and the musket ball. He sealed it off with wax from the burning candle.

"These paper cartridges have all you need for a single shot. Half the gunpowder goes into the pan and the other half in the barrel with the bullet. I'll show you how to load the rifle in a bit," said Will.

"How much gold do we have left over?" said Nate.

"Not a whole lot. We'll have to pull this off with the bullets and letter opener."

"Is there enough to coat those old knuckle dusters?" said Nate.

"Why would you want to do that? Do you think punching them would work?" said Will.

"Why not? Claude Rains beat the shit out of Chaney with just an old cane," said Nate.

"I don't know what the fuck you're talking about, but I'll believe you," said Will, "I guess you could have them as a last resort."

Will dipped the knuckle dusters in the hot crucible. He pulled them out with tongs and dropped them into the bucket. Nate picked them up after they cooled. They were shiny, gold, and ready to punch. He made a couple of jabbing motions and placed them on the table with the bullets.

"Looks like we're all set then," said Nate.

"What now?" said Cody.

"Dinner?" said Will.

The sun was setting and the boys fixed themselves a quick meal of whatever was left in the house. Peanut butter sandwiches, soft taco shells, penne pasta, and bacon. They sat in the living room, looking around the place, waiting for something to happen.

"Should we board up the house, Night of the Living Dead style? I've always wanted to do that," said Cody.

"I've never seen it, but I'm gonna say no. I've got to draw the line somewhere on destroying this house," said Will.

"You've never seen Night of the Living Dead? It's public domain for fucks sake. We could watch it on our goddamn phones."

"Maybe you'd have a job if you spent that time looking for one instead of watching old movies that no one cares about."

"Now's not the time guys," said Nate.

"What's up with all the movie references today?" said Will.

"I don't know. I think it took a few days for us to sync back up," said Nate.

"And now that we are, we're unstoppable," said Cody.

"More like unbearable," said Will.

"It's not our fault that you haven't seen Night of the Living Dead or the Wolf Man. How are we friends?"

"I'm starting to question that myself."

"We could watch one while we wait for those werewolves to show up," said Cody.

"We don't even know if they're going to show up," said Will.

Nate was peeking out from the window up at the sky.

"It's not a full moon tonight anyway," said Nate.

"Shit. Are you fucking kidding me? Are you saying we're going to have to wait an entire month until we get a chance to find them?" said Will.

"I don't know, but I do know it isn't a full moon tonight," said Nate.

The boys were slumped on the couch. A knock came at the door and a woman's voice could be heard behind it.

"We need to talk," said Brett.

"Nothing good has ever come from those words," said Nate.

CHAPTER 10

Will was standing by the door, looking out through the peep hole. Brett, Maya, and Allison were all standing there.

"What do they look like? Are they still human?" said Nate.

"Yeah, they're human. They look like themselves before they turned into chia pets. See I can make references too," said Will.

"Uh huh. So what are they wearing?"

"Who fucking cares what they're wearing, they tried to fucking kill us, Nate!" said Cody.

"I just want to know how good Allison looks."

"Get off the couch if you want to see."

"I'd rather not. I don't want to get too close. She may lure me in with those hypnotic hips."

"You know we can hear you, right?" said Brett, "We've got very sensitive hearing."

The men looked at each other. Cody and Nate jumped to their and joined Will by the door.

"We'll be okay as long as we don't invite them in, right?" said Will.

"Now that's vampires, idiot," said Cody.

"Maybe they'll go away on their own then," said Will.

"I'm going to take one little peek," said Nate.

Nate looked through the door and the women were still there. Brett wore another dress while Allison and Maya were both in tight shorts.

"Jesus, maybe we should let them in here and hear them out," said Nate, "I've got to see that woman up close."

"You're joking, right?"

"Why would I joke about spending another night with the best piece of ass I ever had?"

Nate tossed his eyes from side to side. He was throwing his head towards the stash of gold weapons they had. Will quickly hid the gun and paper cartridges. Cody was beginning to understand and he nodded at Nate in agreement with his plan. Will returned to the others who were still standing at the door.

"I think Nate has the right idea, Will. We should let them in. Brett sure is looking sexy tonight," said Cody.

"A little on the nose, don't you think?" whispered Nate.

"Okay ladies, it looks like I'm outvoted. I'm going to open the door now."

The door swung open and the women mounted themselves there like pillars. Will motioned for them to come inside and they slowly did. The six of them went to the kitchen. There were only three chairs left after last night's events.

"I'd offer you a chair if you didn't break half of them," said Will.

"How about we all stand instead?" said Brett.

"Standing's fine by me," said Cody.

"I'll sit," said Nate.

He took a seat and Allison sat next to him. Brett stood across from Cody while Maya stood closer to Will. The table was still messy from their makeshift dinner. Plates, mugs, forks, and knives covered the top.

"Sorry about the mess. Can I get anyone anything to drink?" said Will.

Everyone shook their heads no.

"Anything to eat?"

"We're what's to eat," said Nate.

"Let's not fuck around here. You're werewolves and you tried to kill us. We assumed you're going to do the same tonight before we saw it wasn't a full moon. Honestly I'm a little taken aback. We thought you liked us," said Cody.

"We do like you," said Brett.

"Ripping off your skin and attacking us isn't what I'd call a good first date. It's not exactly the material I look for in a girlfriend," said Cody.

"I think you boys are confused. We didn't want to kill you. We could have killed you in seconds if we wanted to do that," said Maya.

"Please clarify things for us," said Will, "Cause it didn't seem like you wanted to cuddle."

"We want you to be like us," said Allison, "We wanted to turn you."

"No fucking way. I'm not going to be howling at the moon like a lunatic," said Nate.

"Not to mention all the killing," said Will.

"Yeah, not to mention all the killing too!"

"There's your answer. We're not interested in what you're selling," said Cody.

"Please think about this. We could make you kings. You'll live forever," said Brett.

"And we'll only have to worry about fleas, right?" said Cody.

"You won't ever have to worry about anything ever again."

"I think your offer sucks. I think you were going to eat us. Now I think you're only here because we managed to hurt one of you. You came back either to silence us or offer us this platter of bullshit," said Cody, "Well we're not eating."

"You don't have what it takes to be wolves. You could never stomach it," said Allison.

"Why are we still talking about this? Why don't we kill them now and get it over with?" said Maya.

"You know, we were thinking the same thing. Weren't we boys?" said Nate.

"You fucking know it," said Will, "I'll go get the gold."

"I'm afraid I can't let you do that Will," said Maya.

"See, she can appreciate a good reference," said Cody.

"I'm already way past tired of them," said Will.

"You know, we don't need to be wolves to kill you," said Allison.

"Say goodbye to your friends, Cody," said Brett.

"Excuse me?" said Cody.

Maya grabbed Will by the shirt and carried him off. Allison snatched Nate off his chair and he was gone too. Cody stared down Brett and she locked eyes with him. He could see her eyes flicker yellow for a second.

Maya had taken Will into the living room. She dropped him on the floor and he struggled getting back on his feet. A fist came flying at his face. He ducked to dodge it and returned the favor with a punch of his own. Maya easily moved out of the way.

"You really think you could hit me?" said Maya, "Even if I were a normal human, you wouldn't be able to touch me with that body of yours."

"There's nothing wrong with my body," said Will.

She sent another jab his way and he took it in the chin. He staggered backwards and sent a sideways kick to Maya. She hopped away from it without breaking a sweat. Will crouched down and ran at Maya. He tackled into her and they plummeted to the ground near the fireplace. She shifted, getting on top of her prey. She held her hands around his neck and squeezed. His own hand reached out, smacking the woman on top of him. It was little use. She didn't budge.

He stretched his hands out around him looking for something grab onto. His fingers felt something. It was cold. It was metal. He grabbed the fire poker and slammed it into Maya's torso. It broke the bind her hands had on his neck. She fell to the side and he panted as he climbed over her. He raised the fire iron into the air and drove it through her left eye socket. Her limbs flailed and stopped as he twisted the poker in her head. Blood poured out like a geyser onto the floorboards.

Will crawled to the couch and tried to catch his breath.

Allison had carried Nate outside. They were in front of the house by Nate's truck. She let him down gently before slashing at him with a knife she took from the kitchen.

"Is it too late to change my mind about this?" said Nate.

He ducked the knife and looked around to see what he could defend himself with. Gravel filled the driveway and he hurled pieces of stone at Allison. She laughed it off while stabbing towards him again. She barely missed his stomach, slicing a horizontal hole through his shirt for proof.

"We only wanted you and your friends to share our gift," said Allison.

"Some gift. Did you act like this before you started shedding regularly?" said Nate.

"I thought I liked your weirdness at first, but now it's annoying."

She swung again and he grabbed her wrist. He squeezed with his left hand while sending a right hook into Allison's face. She dropped the knife and sunk to her knees. Nate picked the blade up and skewered the knife into Allison's throat. She gasped and fell over to her side.

Cody and Brett were locked in a staring contest as they heard the sounds of the others fighting. She ran her fingers through her short red hair and smiled, breaking the eye contact. Cody watched her running at him with a mug in her hands. She swung it at him, missing and the mug shattered on a counter top. Cody grabbed a mug of his own and threw it at her head. It smashed on the floor and they both grabbed for more. She chucked one and it broke. He swung one and it only hit the fridge. They circled around the table, each trying to predict the other one's moves. Brett jumped onto the table, slid across it with a mug heading for Cody's noggin. He went low and grabbed Brett by her torso, slamming her onto the table.

She looked up at him and grinned.

"You could have been king," she said.

"That sounds like too much responsibility," he said.

He smashed two mugs into her head. Her body went limp.

Cody climbed off the table and called out to his friends.

"Will? Nate? Are you alright?"

He heard Will's voice from the living room. He sounded winded.

"I'm in here. I think I killed Maya," he said.

Cody carried Brett's body into the living room. Maya was laying in a small pool of her blood. He placed Brett's body next to hers and he took a seat on the couch next to Will. Nate pushed through the front door. Allison's body was in his arms. He looked at the boys then at the women on the floor before placing Allison with them. He joined his friends on the sofa and they sat in silence for a minute.

"We fucking killed them. I can't believe we killed them," said Will.

"I can't believe it worked. I guess they die the same as us when they are us," said Nate.

"What the fuck do we do? What do we tell the cops?" said Cody.

"I don't know. I mean, we're not murderers. They were werewolves!" said Nate.

"We've got time to think about what we'll tell the cops. At least it's all over now," said Will.

Moonlight shined down on the bodies from the living room window. The women's bodies began to change once more.

"You just had to go and say something," said Nate, "I can't believe this shit."

"We should be filming this for the internet," said Cody.

"Are you insane? We'd be locked away from by some alphabet agency before it was ever seen by the public."

"You think the government already knows about werewolves?"

"Absolutely."

"Why don't we call them for help then?"

"Because they'll lock us away for even finding out about them or they'd try to discredit us for mentioning it."

Fur quickly replaced the girls' wounded skin which flaked off their bodies. Their hands and feet turned to paws. Torsos thickened, clothes ripped, and tails sprung out.

"I don't understand. Why are they changing? It isn't a full moon tonight," said Nate.

"Wait, a minute. It wasn't a full moon last night either," said Cody.

"Are you sure? It looked pretty full to me," said Will.

"I'm looking at a moon app on my phone right now," said Cody, "It hasn't been a full moon in nearly five days."

"What does that mean?" said Nate.

"I think these bitches transform every night is what that means," said Cody.

"White, they're only weak to gold, and they turn into monsters every night? Sure, why not?" said Nate.

CHAPTER 11

The women were fully transformed into their wolf forms. They laid on the floor with their human skins peeled off them, barely clinging on. Their furry chests were breathing, but they weren't moving. And their eyes were shut tight. The boys stood around them in awe, barely moving themselves.

"Why are we standing around doing nothing? Go get the gun and we can kill them while they're knocked out or sleeping or whatever the fuck is going on," said Nate.

"Alright, let's do this," said Will, "Let's go together."

"You and Cody go, I'll stay here and keep watch," said Nate.

"Keep watch? Over sleeping werewolves? And what happens when they wake up?" said Cody.

"I haven't thought that far ahead yet," said Nate.

"C'mon, Cody, we'll be quick," said Will.

Will led the way and they headed upstairs to Cody's room. Inside was the gun, the crucible, and letter opener. They were laying on the bed looking like clothes to be put on after a shower.

"Why'd you put all this shit in here?" said Cody.

"It had to go somewhere, didn't it?" said Will.

"Aren't we missing something? Where are the knucks at?"

"I don't think Nate's taken them out of his pocket since we dipped them in gold. He probably thinks I'll let him keep them after all this is over."

"Are you going to?"

"Maybe I'll surprise him with them as a birthday present."

Cody grabbed the letter opener, tossing it in his hands like he had seen Nate do. He whipped it around, plunging it through the air. He threw it up again and it slipped out of his hands. It landed on the bed and he could see Aconite still hanging there proudly.

"We should have dipped the damn sword in gold," said Cody, "It'd probably chop their heads clean off."

"Yeah if you were willing to give up that necklace of yours or Shannon's or whoever you plan on giving it to," said Will.

"I'm sorry if I've been an asshole lately. Life hasn't been exactly easy for me these days. I'm trying to stay positive, but it's hard when the last woman you slept with turns out to be a creature of the night."

"You're fine. I know it's hard to lose your job and then your girlfriend. If anything, I've been cold to you. I should be more supportive. Call me out on it if I'm not."

"Alright then, let's kill these things, have some beers, and make amends."

"We pull this off and I'll even watch those shitty horror movies you like so much."

"It's a deal."

"I hope I remember how to do this right."

Will began loading the black powder rifle. He held it longways to start, opening the pan on the gun. Next he took out one of the paper cartridges from his pocket, tearing it open and pouring some of the gun powder into the rifle. He closed the pan, turned the rifle upward and dumped the rest of the powder, ball and paper into the barrel. He slipped out of the ramrod from the side and used it to push the contents further down into the barrel. He returned the ramrod to its place and fully cocked the gun.

"You have to do that every time?" said Cody.

"Only if you want it to shoot," said Will.

Footsteps stampeded up the stairs towards the room. Nate burst in, slamming the door behind him, and breathing heavily. Another set of footsteps were heard following the same path.

"She's right behind me," said Nate, "Get ready to shoot the bitch."

"Which one is it?" said Will.

"It's yours, Will," said Nate.

Bits of wood flew through the air as the door smashed open. The boys quickly jumped behind the bed, crouching down with the gun aimed up. The Maya-wolf burst into the room with teeth baring. She jumped onto the bed and looked down at the prey in front of her. Her snout snarled and it looked like the beast were laughing.

"You see this shit? She's laughing. This bastard is fucking laughing at us. They fucking knew they couldn't be killed as humans. They were toying with us and we bought it," said Nate.

"Shoot it, Will!" said Cody, "Blow its head off."

Will, raised the rifle, pulled the trigger and the ball whizzed by the wolf, landing in the ceiling. The Maya-wolf's snarling mouth only grew bigger.

"You flinched. All that talk about not flinching and you flinched, dammit," said Nate.

"No I didn't!" said Will.

Cody wasn't having any part of the argument. He was too busy lunging at the wolf with the letter opener in his hand. He aimed for the wolf's heart. He didn't make it. His leap was met with a swipe of a paw, sending him into the wall and collapsing onto the floor. The wolf turned back towards Nate and Will.

"Hurry up and reload," said Nate.

Will grabbed another paper cartridge from his pocket, tore it open, poured half in the pan. He tilted the gun to access the barrel and the rest of the gun powder scattered all over the floor. He nearly had tears in his eyes as he looked at Nate.

"God dammit, why couldn't you keep a real gun in the house?" said Nate, "Looks like I'll have to do it myself."

He had the knuckle dusters in his hand when he jumped onto the bed. The Maya-wolf swiped a claw and Nate bobbed out of the way. Another two paw punches came at him and he ducked one while just barely dodging the other. He could feel the wind off the claw on that last one. He planted his feet, got low, and popped up with an uppercut. The golden punch landed squarely on the beast's snowy snout. The Maya-wolf wobbled and dropped on the bed.

"It worked," said Nate looking towards Will and Cody.

Cody was dusting himself off, using the wall to stand until Will gave him a hand. The wolf was out cold in front of them.

"I can't believe it. I really can't believe it," said Will.

"I told you it'd work," said Nate.

"I never doubted it," said Cody.

Cody picked up the letter opener and climbed onto the bed. He felt someone grab his shoulder. It was Will.

"Let me do it," he said.

"Are you sure?"

"She was 'mine' wasn't she? It's only right I take care of this. Don't worry, I'll let you get your chance to clean up your mess," said Will.

He took the letter opener from Cody and knelt over the werewolf. He sent it down into her chest, impaling the heart. Its yellow eyes popped open, howling in pain. The Maya-wolf's white fur was turning red from blood.

"That's one down. Two to go," said Will.

In one final breath her claws swiped at Will and they pierced his chest. Her howl trailed off, her eyes dimmed, and Will went quiet.

He hopped off the bed and the guys could see the blood trickling from Will's chest. It was torn wide open. Bits of muscle, skin, and flesh trailing behind him. He slumped down by the dresser and laid his head on it.

"Will?"

Nate was kneeling by him. Will looked up and he had let those tears run now. Cody grabbed a pillow and held it firmly against Will's chest.

"I'm so sorry guys. I didn't think she was going to do that," he said.

Nate held his hand tight. Cody's pillow was filling with blood.

"You don't have anything to be sorry about. You didn't do anything wrong," said Nate.

"But the house. My parents are going to be so pissed at me," he said.

"I think they'll understand."

"I hope so. I really do. Cause I had a lot of fun seeing you guys again and I'd like to make a habit of it."

"We're not going anywhere, but how about you get some rest, buddy," said Nate, "We'll take care of the others."

"That sounds good. I think I will."

He craned his head down and his eyes went still. His breathing stopped and Cody removed the pillow. Will was gone.

"Why you'd have to go and get yourself killed Will," said Nate.

He was hanging onto his dead friend while Cody stood up.

"What the hell have we got ourselves into Nate?" said Cody, "She fucking killed him."

"What'd you think was going to happen tonight? Did you think we were going to slay some werewolves without any danger? Will knew what the stakes were," said Nate.

"Still. It feels too real. I can't believe he's gone. We were just starting to open up to each other again. I mean literally five minutes before he died."

"We won't let his death be in vain. We're going to kill those things down there and then we're going to give Will the greatest funeral of all time," said Nate.

"You get the gun, I'll get the dagger."

"Letter opener."

"It's been promoted."

Cody slipped the letter opener out from the wolf's chest. He paused for a moment with the blade held in a striking position. He waited for the wolf to pop up and bite him. It didn't. It laid there with Will laying nearby. Two one night lovers dead together in a beach house.

Nate grabbed the four remaining paper cartridges from Will's pocket. He slipped them into his own and stood up by Cody. The two friends hugged. Neither wanting to break the embrace. But they had to. There was work to be done and they were the only men up for it. Nate picked up the rifle and faux aimed it around.

"Do you know how to load it?" said Cody.

"Only from watching the Patriot," said Nate.

"Oh great so we're depending on Mel Gibson now."

"You're the one that watched Will load," said Nate, "Are you sure you want me to shoot it? Wouldn't it make more sense for you to use it?"

"You're a better shot than me. That blast would only make me miss. How about this? I'll stand by and walk you through it."

They headed back down to the living room. Brett and Allison were still laying there as beasts with their skins draped around them.

"Okay how do I do it?" said Nate.

"It's easy. Hold the gun parallel. Now open the pan," said Cody.

"What's the pan?"

"That metal flap thing,"

"Okay."

He shifted the gun into position.

"Good so far. Next, pour in half the gun powder."

Nate's teeth tore open the paper cartridge.

"Now close the pan, shift the gun upright. Pour in the ball, the gun powder and stuff in the paper into the barrel."

Nate did so and looked at Cody for affirmation.

"One last thing is jam it tight with the metal rod thing."

Nate pushed down the rod and returned it to its place.

"That's it?"

"That's it. Except fully cock it. And you're ready to go."

The werewolves bodies were beginning to twitch. Slices of yellow were starting to show through their eyelids. Their clawed hands were opening and closing.

"Alright, you taught me how to reload it. Now get out of here. They're waking up. "

"I'm not going anywhere. We're in this together. I'm not going to hide while you risk your life," said Cody.

"Yes you are. I'm not going to let these bitches kill you like they did Will. Not get out of here and I'll call you when it's over. Go hide in the dumb waiter," said Nate.

"Are you sure? I don't want you think I'm a coward."

"I'd never think that."

Cody turned to head down the hallway. He heard Nate's voice beckon him back.

"One more thing. You know I love you right?" said Nate.

"I love you too man," said Cody.

CHAPTER 12

Nate held the rifle firmly in his hands in the beach house living room. He had it aimed at the head of the woman who he was sleeping with only a night ago. Next to her lay another woman who his friend was with. But they weren't women. Not really. They were wolves and they were awake. And he had hesitated to pull the trigger.

The Allison-wolf swung a paw at Nate, pushing him back into the sofa. He landed on his ass and kept his gun pointed on the wolf. The other wolf, Brett hop to her feet, sniffed the air and took off out of sight. Allison charged Nate and he fired his rifle. It went off with a loud pop and he jerked the stock at the last moment. The musket round went into the fireplace. The werewolf was untouched. Not a hair was out of place. It let out a short howl and Nate roared back.

He had his golden knuckles hanging in his fingers and met the running beast in the middle of their distance. The wolf was faster, gaining ground before Nate could find his footing. Allison snapped her jaws at Nate, chomping at air as he tried to avoid being a midnight snack. Large daggers jutted out of her snout and Nate could smell death whenever she opened her mouth. He sent a direct jab into the wolf's gut. His punch sent the beast backwards and now it was his turn to gain ground on her. The white wolf howled as she sent a white pawed kick at Nate. It connected into his torso and burst the wind out of him. *Breathe, got to breathe. And I've got to find cover. I need to find a place to reload that stupid gun.* He held his stance and twisted his body to avoid another furry kick. Nate clutched the knuckles, squared up with Allison and sent a jab right between her eyes. There was never a cleaner punch between man and wolf.

She wobbled, but didn't fall. Nate could see the stars whizzing around the beast's head. He grabbed the gun and bolted down the hallway. There was only one bedroom on the first floor, Will's room or rather his parents'. The door opened with a light push and he slammed it behind him. Nate examined where he was. The bed was still messy, clothes were on the floor, and picture frames were hung on the walls and sitting on the dresser. He pushed the dresser in front of the door and couldn't help but glance at the photos. One was of a young Will standing on the beach holding a crab in his hands. *He looked so happy as a child. I'm so sorry I couldn't save you.* Nate could almost hear Will's ghost yelling at him for flinching when pulling the trigger. He put the frame down and another caught his eye. Three young men were looking back at him. They were on the boardwalk near a concession stand. *We should have gone to the damn boardwalk again instead of a nude beach.*

He put the photo back and let out a wet cough. His hand wiped his mouth and there was blood on it. Nate took a deep breath and winced with pain. The only thing keeping him from collapsing was holding onto the dresser as a crutch. He felt his torso and gently touched his ribs. His fingers went flying back from the pain. Barely touching his chest sent spikes of pain as if he were being electrocuted. He let out a cry and forced his fingers to go back down. The shivers of pain started at the top of his ribs. He coughed again and more blood came up. *Damn bitch got me good with that kick. She must have broken at least two of my ribs.*

I can't waste any more time. I need to kill these werewolves, grab Cody and get to a hospital. Oh God, it hurts so fucking bad. I've got to fight through the pain. Got to keep going.

He pushed himself to the bed with the rifle in hand. Every bit of movement seemed to send more blood up his throat. It gurgled inside him. Every breath was more strenuous. *Feels like I'm drowning.* The sounds of footsteps were ringing through the house. The wolf was hunting him and he knew it.

The rifle sat at his side. He opened the latch and ripped another paper cartridge. The powder poured in and he closed it. *I hope I'm doing this right. I can't afford to miss again.*

The gun slid down the bed, letting him access the barrel. He poured the rest of the powder, musket ball and paper inside. *My head sure feels funny. Weird, isn't it?* The metal rod pushed down the contents of the barrel and brought the rifle back up as though he were climbing a rope. He held it in his hands, fully cocked and finger near the trigger. He looked at the photo on the dresser again. *Who knew we'd end up like this, eh Will?* His other hand clutched the golden knuckle dusters and he was ready for a fight. *Okay here's the plan: Allison bursts in and you shoot her. No one could fuck that up, right? Except me, the first time.* He let out a whistle, blowing out vapors of blood as he did so. But it did the trick.

The sound of footsteps headed towards the room. *That's it, take the bait. Come here so I can shoot your furry heart out.*

The wolf was upon the room in seconds. Nate's breathing was getting heavier, slower, and more painful with every draw of air. He tried taking deeper long breaths, but that did little good. He was bleeding out and he knew it. The dresser was still blocking the door and it budged when the beast smacked from the hallway. The room itself shook and the bed he was braced against rippled. His ribs quaked and it seemed to loosen more fluids.

The door shook once more. Cracks formed in the top half. Shards of wood flaked off onto the dresser below. Another push and another chunk of door fell. Nate tried to keep calm. His legs and fingers were shaking instead. A quick 'roo' came from the other side before the top half of the door splintered. Claws pushed through widening the newly formed holes. He held the rifle up. There wasn't a clear shot of the beast. Then there was. The Allison-wolf pushed it's body through the hole and the door broke completely. Her white furry body climbed over the dresser and was ten feet within Nate. *Not yet, I could still miss. No, dammit, take the shot. Don't psyche yourself out.*

His legs quaked. He was off the bed and barely holding the rifle. The wolf stared at him. Its yellow eyes squinting. Its nose sniffing. Its tongue licking its bear trap teeth. She knew he was bleeding. She could smell and see it all over him. Her prey was injured.

Nate screamed into the air, throwing a jab and hitting nothing. The wolf sent a backhanded paw in response. He fell to the bed, picking himself up and wanting to vomit. His vision was going haywire. Everything had an outline to it. And there were two of them. Two dressers, two wolves, two guns when he looked down. His eyes felt on fire and the smallest of glances left or right felt sent pain down his spine.

I can't wait any longer. I've got to shoot it. Got to make sure Cody's safe.

The wolf was done playing and lorded over Nate. He lifted the rifle and it was inches away from the beast. He pulled the trigger. It sent out a pop, but no bang. *A dud? Are you fucking kidding me?*

Allison picked him up and sneered. Nate could see the drool oozing down from her jaws. Her claws were digging into his sides and the ribs were a mere paper cut compared to the pain he felt now. The gun was still in his hands, aimed towards the massive wolf in front of him. She squeezed him tighter and he screamed with blood dribbling down the sides of his mouth. Then the rifle finally went off.

A loud pop rang out through the bedroom. The golden musket ball freed itself from the barrel and hit Allison's large canine face. The ball went from under the snout into the back of the wolf's head. It hit the brain and her entire head popped. The gun had hang fired. Nate was free from her grip. The headless werewolf dropped to the floor with a thud. He turned grabbed the gun by its stock, pointed the barrel down and used it to stabilize himself.

"God bless the second amendment. God Bless America. Fuck you King George," he shouted.

Nate pushed himself to the dresser and called out to his friend.

"I got her, Code, I got her!"

Cody came running out from his hiding spot and he could see his friend through the torn door. Nate was holding onto the dresser like it were a life raft. Cody had to rip pieces of wood out to get through. He climbed over the furniture, looked at the dead wolf with no head and saw his buddy covered in blood.

"Jesus, Nate, what the fuck happened? Are you alright?"

"I got her, but she didn't go easy. I think she broke a few ribs."

Cody gently pushed the dresser to the side and offered a shoulder to Nate. Nate took it and let Cody take most of his weight. They headed back to the living room, each step leading to a low groan from Nate. His breathing was raspy. His throat sounded clogged and he could barely walk.

"I've got to get you out of here. Do you have your keys on you?"

"Always. Except we're not going anywhere."

"You're going to die unless we leave right now."

"We still have work to do Code. We need to kill the other one first. Then we can go."

"We're leaving. Fuck the other one."

"You already did."

"Stop joking around. I'm going to get you help."

They had reached the living room and Nate pushed away to sit on the couch. Cody tried pulling him back to his feet and Nate declined his hand.

"I can't help, but keep thinking the same thing. Maybe we wouldn't be in this mess if none of us used our brains to think instead of dicks."

"No one could have known they were werewolves, Nate."

"Yeah, maybe you're right."

"Come on, let's go."

"Don't worry about me, Code. I'll be good. I just need a few minutes to rest."

"I'm going to get you an ice pack for those ribs."

Nate let himself laugh and he shivered with pain.

"I think we're beyond the ice pack."

Cody headed to the fridge and there was no ice to be found. He grabbed a clean wash rag and wet it with cold water. He ran back to the living room and he could see yellow eyes staring down at him from the between the railings of the banister.

"We've got to go, right now," said Cody, "Brett's right upstairs."

He held his hand out and Nate grabbed it. Cody pulled him to his feet and the eyes moved in a flash. The beast jumped off the banister and landed between the two men. She turned and snarled at Cody. She raised a claw and swung it, keeping her eyes locked on her lover. Her paw swept and Nate's head flew off his body. It landed in the fire place. The Brett-wolf threw back her head, her claws raised into the air, and let out a long howl.

"Nate! No!" screamed Cody.

CHAPTER 13

The world halted to a pause. The house had gone quiet. The only sound were the light waves crashing in the backyard's beach. Cody's heart was beating faster than he knew was possible. Brett's eyes were locked on him. They shined like stars and he could nearly see other worlds locked inside them. He broke the staring contest first.

Cody went for the rifle and the wolf beat him to it. Brett picked it up with her paws and tore the barrel apart with a mixture of tooth and claw. Metal and wood rained on the ground. The wolf turned back and leaned down at the man. Her nostrils flared, wetting his face, and he could hear her growl. Her eyes were fixated on the golden necklace he wore around his neck.

He closed his eyes tight, waiting for the beast to devour him. Five long seconds passed and nothing happened. A scraping sound caused him to open his eyes again. But it wasn't the sound of his flesh being ripped from his bones. Cody was untouched.

The scraping sound was that of the Brett-wolf dragging Nate's headless corpse across the floor. His head laid by the fireplace with his mouth wide open in fear. Cody covered his own mouth and the vomit flowed anyway.

I've got to get out of here. I've got to far away from here.

There was something shining in the moonlight on the floorboards. Nate's truck keys had fell out of his pocket almost immediately when she moved him. Cody grabbed them and looked towards the front door. Two yellow lights hovered there as sentries. Brett was wedging her snout full of

Nate at the main entrance. She paused to smile at Cody with pieces of his friend stuck in her teeth.

That fucking bitch. She knows what she's doing. She's doing this to taunt me. Nate, I'm so sorry. I'm going to live for you and Will, but first I've got to find another way out. She thinks she can keep me in here? Fuck that. I'll jump from the second floor into the water if I have to.. But I've got to be quiet. I can't let that thing hear where I'm headed.

The two remaining paper cartridges were now in Cody's possession. *Little good they'll do me without a gun.* He shoved them in his pocket while he headed for the dumb waiter. Seems he and the waiter had become good friends during his stay in Holborn. He climbed in, pulled himself up and was back in his guest room.

Will's lifeless body looked cold and Cody didn't want to touch him to find out. The Maya-wolf was still dead on the bed and that damn sword still hung over it. Cody started to laugh. *At least that sword didn't budge during all this.*

Cody opened the doors to the balcony and stepped outside. The moon, although not full, was still providing plenty of light in the night. The water was jump's away and Cody looked back into the room again. He could hear Will and Nate telling him to hurry up and get out of there. But he didn't. He went inside and grabbed the sword off the wall.

Then he lit the crucible with the burner and swung the sword around while it got hot. The paper cartridges ripped open and he tossed in the golden musket rounds. Cody put on the gloves and had the tongs on the side, ready to grab the melted gold.

It's you and me now Aconite. We're going to cut a bitch.

The small rounds in the crucible weren't much. Cody got down on his hands and knees, feeling around the room. *Jackpot!* He found the round that hit the wall and the other that Will dropped to the floor. He added them into the pot and a pool of gold formed. *This isn't enough. I need more. I've got to find more.* Then he looked down at himself. *Fine.*

He removed the golden chain from his neck and relinquished it into the crucible. It quickly melted in with the rest of the gold. There was enough now.

How am I going to do this? Even if I pour it on, won't I need to sharpen it? It won't cut anything without being sharpened. Or maybe it'll work. Maybe it's some bullshit werewolf magic crap that I don't understand. I don't think I have many options left to try. I may as well leave an interesting corpse for those cops to find.

He used the tongs to pick up the crucible and tilted it over the sword. Gold poured over the blade. The pot emptied and the weapon was covered. The crucible fell to the floor with a thud. Cody picked up the golden sword by the hilt. Pieces of gold dripped and he knew he fucked up. *I don't have anything to cool it. God dammit.*

Cody ran out onto the balcony to drop the sword into the water below. It hit with a confirming sound of extinguishing heat. He counted to three before following it down. The ocean welcomed him with a cold splash. He swam to where he tossed the sword and reached into the sands. He came up empty handed.

He was drenched, he was freezing, he was tired. A howl shocked him back to reality. Brett was standing on the balcony letting out a long call to the moon. Her claws were flexing in the wind, her tail wagging, and those horrible eyes scanning for Cody. She howled again before plunging into the ocean.

Cody's eyes were now scanning for the wolf. He had seen her jump in, but she hadn't surfaced. His hands rummaged below in vain attempts to find the sword.

He hands felt something. It wasn't metal. It was soft. It was *fur*. Cody pulled and the wolf rose from the depths. His hand was on her tail. He jumped back into the waves with Brett in pursuit. The beast was roaring at him. Cody swam, arm over arm, not sure where to go. Then he saw he wasn't going anywhere. Brett grabbed his leg and held him in place. His arms flailed going nowhere. She dragged him under water before pulling him into the air. Her eyes narrowed. Her brow furrowed. Her mouth opened. And she bit.

Her teeth tore into Cody's shoulder. His skin tore open, blood gushing out, and he screamed at the sky. The wolf lifted Cody over her head and tossed him back into the ocean. His mind was spinning along with his world. He was tumbling head over feet in the water. His hands felt all around him, trying to protect his skull from being hit. He felt the sands below, he reached out and touched something else too. It was metal.

He kept a firm grip on the metal to make sure it stayed in his hands as he surfaced. The air felt good. His shoulder did not. He lifted his arm and it looked even longer with the sword in hand. The gold shined brightly from the moon. Aconite was ready for a fight.

The wolf charged him. She swung a paw and he swung the sword back. Her claws fell into the ocean. Brett howled in pain and clenched at her bleeding wrist. She leaned forward, lowering her height to Cody's and snapped her jaws at him. A few of his hairs were torn from his head as he dodged the last chomp.

He dove under the water and headed for shore. Brett settled for him reaching the shallows. She had grabbed him again, pulling him to his feet with one hand left. He felt his arm going weak from blood loss. They locked eyes for the last time. She snarled and howled at the man before her.

"You killed my friends and you were terrible in bed!"

Cody held the golden sword high and swung it. It landed between the wolf's eyes, splitting the head open. And it didn't stop there. Aconite went all the way down Brett's torso. Cody had torn the beast in two. Two equal halves plopped onto the beach. The yellow eyes dimmed fast.

Cody braced himself with the sword and headed for the front of the house. He managed to make while only stumbling three times.

Cody opened the front door. Nate's half eaten corpse greeted him. There was hardly anything left beyond his legs. He reached into his friend's pocket and pulled out his wallet. He slipped out the card that the cops had given them. Then he grabbed Nate's phone and dialed the number.

It rang five times until a sleepy voice answered. It sounded disoriented and it sounded familiar.

"Hello? May I ask who's calling?"

"Officer Dunne?"

"Yes, that's me."

"I'm Cody Walker. You pulled my friend over about my fight with Gordon. Do you remember?"

"Yes, I remember who you and your friends are. Is there something wrong, Mr. Walker? Or did you want to interrupt my sleep to chit chat? Maybe you wanted to see if the number really worked. Well it does."

"I know you won't believe me, but these women who turned out to be werewolves killed my friends. I know it sounds crazy. And even if you don't believe me, I'm bleeding bad. I need an ambulance. "

"We've been looking for those damn werewolves for a week now. You found them? Where are they now?"

"We killed them."

"Hang tight Cody. We're on our way."

Cody gave the address and sat on the steps. His shoulder wasn't taking it easy on letting the blood leak. More and more poured out as though he had an infinite supply. He tore off his wet shirt, cutting strips with the sword and wrapping them around his shoulder diagonally. He tied it off tight and stuck the sword into the stairs. He rested his head on the hilt.

Minutes passed before flashing lights came flying down the road. It was the first time Cody could remember being happy seeing those blues and reds.

The cops hopped out of their car. It was the mustache and bald head; Naughton and Dunne. They had long revolvers at their sides. Cody rose to his feet with the sword in his hands.

"We see you figured out how to kill them," said Naughton.

"Yeah gold seems to do the trick," said Cody.

"Why didn't you call us for help sooner?" said Dunne.

"Yeah those werewolves were doing a number on this town," said Naughton.

"If you knew they were werewolves around then what was that shit implying I killed Gordon?"

"Just because there's werewolves doesn't mean regular folk aren't going around carving people up. We needed to check all angles," said Naughton, "And we couldn't come out and tell you we think a werewolf killed Gordon. You would have thought we were nuts."

Cody nodded his head.

"Usually people take the hint and let us know is something weird is going on. I guess you and your friends aren't very trusting of the police," said Dunne.

"Do you blame us? If you were regular cops then you would have thought we were the crazy ones."

"That's true."

"Wait a second. Did you say 'usually'? You mean werewolves regularly attack people here?"

"Nah. It's not only werewolves. Vampires, ghouls, fishmen from the deep. All sorts of weird shit," said Naughton.

"I am never ever coming back to Holborn."

"We don't blame you, but we're glad you're okay. I'm guessing your friends-" said Dunne.

"They didn't make it. We made a pretty big mess of things in there. Both sides shed their share of blood."

"Don't worry. We'll explain this to the authorities. You're going to be okay Cody Walker. Everything is going to be okay," said Naughton.

An ambulance pulled up moments later. The EMTs helped Cody inside and he collapsed still holding the golden blade in his hands.

CHAPTER 14

The last few weeks of summer always go by so fast. Warm weather is replaced with a chilly breeze before anyone can figure out what happened. The green leaves turn a beautiful color then wither to nothing and it occurs before most ever notice. Nearly four weeks had gone by since the incident at the Holborn beach house.

The cover story told to the families of Nate and Will along with anyone who asked was simple. A deranged serial killer was on the prowl in Holborn. This killer, a male, went on a rampage killing over eight people. Cody Walker was the sole survivor and hailed as bringing the murder spree to an end. He had called officers Naughton and Dunne who shot the killer. Thus freeing Cody from any hard pressed hero questions and any trial he'd have to go to on account of a self defense manslaughter charge.

"You understand why you can't tell people the truth, right?" said Dunne.

"Because you're rather think people are safe to walk the streets at night? Because the world isn't ready to know that werewolves are out there and ready to kill them at a moment's notice?"

"That puts it pretty nicely, Cody. Maybe you should work for us," said Naughton.

"I'm guessing that's invitation for you to keep a closer eye on me. Make sure I don't tell anyone anything."

"That's a part of it. Another is we could always use another set of hands," said Dunne.

"I appreciate the offer, but I think I've fought enough monsters for one lifetime."

"Hey if you change your mind-"

"Yes, I have your card and number."

This was one of many conversations Cody had with the officers while he spent a couple days in a hospital. The doctors did the standard tests, ran the standard exams and sewed up his shoulder. He was fine from what the doctors could tell. And Cody could tell they weren't regular doctors by the way they dressed and by the lack of ID tags. They wanted to remain nameless and any personal questions were played off. They kept him there for three nights as if they were waiting for a magic trick to happen. Nothing did and he was sent back to his apartment.

It was as he had left it. Trash everywhere and an absolute disgrace. *It's time to clean this up.* And he did. He cleaned for an entire day, making it look presentable and neat. The next day he spent sending out applications. The next week he spent going to job interviews. The week after that he started his new job. It was part time and it was in an office, but it was a start back to a normal life. Something he should have done without having to see his friends be killed by werewolves. The days became easier, but nights seemed to get worse.

Every night he dreamed that he was back in the beach house. Nate and Will were calling his name. Begging him to save them. He tried to run, but his legs wouldn't move. He cried into the night and it turned into a howl. That howl brought on the women. They rushed him, running on all fours, covered in their white fur and clacking their jaws. He'd start to sink into the ground and he could see Nate and Will rising into the sky. The werewolves would reach him and pull him out of the ground only to start eating his legs, arms, and face.

Cody woke up in his bed. He was home. He was safe. He'd been having these nightmares for weeks now. They happened every single night since it all went down. Those ghosts haunted him constantly. Not only his friends, but the spirits of the wolves he had slaughtered. He felt guilty and that guilt kept him from having a good night's rest.

Cody tried to remember one of the conversations he had while in the hospital. The nightmares started there on the first night while he still under full time surveillance. He woke up, covered in sweat, and screaming. Dunne and Naughton were sitting in a corner, ready for anything.

"Having a nightmare?" said Dunne.

"Was it that obvious?" said Cody.

"Is it something you want to talk about?" said Naughton.

"Not particularly. I think you might have a good idea."

"Okay well I've dealt with many cases survivor's guilt. Myself included. I want to tell you that what happened wasn't your fault. You boys went through hell in that house. You went through something I wouldn't wish on anyone. You did the best you could to save them and you have to make peace with that fact," said Naughton.

"Don't feel bad about killing those werewolves either," said Dunne.

"That's going to be hard. I feel pretty shitty about it. They were women after all."

"Try to think about this way. Would you feel bad about killing a zombie?" said Naughton.

"Well, no, but-"

"No buts. Think of these things as zombies that can talk and claw your face off," said Dunne.

"They're a plague like zombies, Cody. Hell they're worse because they can disguise themselves. You don't see zombies out there trying to seduce men. You did the right thing. Don't lose sleep over it," said Naughton

"I'm still going to be lose sleep over losing my friends."

"That we can't help you with. All I can say is I'm sorry for you loss," said Dunne.

"It's going to take time, Cody," said Naughton.

"How much time?"

"It depends on the person and how easily they can forgive themselves," said Naughton.

"How long did the nightmares last for you?"

"In our line of work? They never go away," said Naughton.

"But you know what helps?" said Dunne.

"I'm all ears."

"Keep moving forward. Occupy your time and mind."

"You want me to distract myself and pretend nothing happened?"

"Would you rather fall into a state of depression? Feeling sorry for yourself and spending the rest of your life wondering 'what if' and bullshit like that?"

Cody decided to give it a try. He forced himself to get up early and try to live his life as normal as possible. He got home from work late in the evening. He cooked himself a meal and relaxed on the couch. He cried while watching Night of the Living Dead. The sun sunk and he was alone in his apartment once more. But tonight that didn't last long. The doorbell rang and he answered it. It was her. Shannon in all her glory, ringing Cody Walker's doorbell. *She sure knows how to wear a dress even when it's almost fall.*

"Are you going to let me in or would you rather me freeze so you can lick me later?" she said.

"How about I let you in and we'll see about the licking," said Cody.

"It feels so good to be back together, baby," said Shannon.

They had resumed their relationship soon after the funerals. She claimed she missed him more than ever and that his friends' deaths made her realize that 'we can go at any time' and 'that we should love each other while we can.' He obliged her and they'd been seeing each other nearly every other day.

He stepped outside and kissed her deep, looking up at the night sky. The moon shined high in the night. It was the first full moon since the attack. He held her close, feeling the goosebumps on her thighs as she shivered.

"We better continue this inside," said Cody.

They made love in his room. Cody had done some minor redecorating. Will's parents had allowed him to keep the sword, Aconite. They didn't understand why the serial killer had dipped it in gold or why Cody would want to keep it after what he had been through. Still they let him have it and he hung it over his bed. Will's father wouldn't let him take it until he told him the meaning of the name, Aconite; wolf's bane. *If he only knew.*

He rolled over to his side and kissed her. She tasted sweet.

"The sword's a little tacky, isn't it?" she said, "It looks like it's going to fall down on us in the middle of the night."

They had fallen asleep. There was no nightmare tonight, but Cody woke up anyway. He clutched at his stomach. It made a loud gurgle and he felt like he had to vomit. He sat up on the edge of the bed. The moon lit up his room and it the sudden movement had woken Shannon.

"Are you okay Cody?" she said.

"I'm fine, I think I just need some water."

"Okay, hurry back. We should take advantage of us both being up so late."

A glass of water later and his stomach felt no better. And worse the pain had spread to his head. He fell to his knees and rubbed at his temples. *Those idiots. Those fucking bastards. They thought I was sick. They thought I had it. And they were right. I understand it now. Only men transform on during a full moon.*

His thighs bulked out, his torso twisted and his skin was peeling of his body. A sound poured out from his throat as though he were choking on his saliva. Cody pushed himself off the ground onto his feet. He felt taller. He felt stronger. He felt like he was able to take on the entire world.

He sniffed the air. Everything smelled different now. His long tongue licked at his longer teeth.

Cody looked down at his hands. To call them that would be a lie. They were paws and they were covered in dark fur. He caught a glimpse of himself in a mirror. He had become what he hated. He was jet black and seven feet tall with a tail. The fur on his back stuck up like needles upon seeing himself. He smashed his claws against the mirror, sending shards all over the floor. His stomach started to gurgle again.

So hungry. Must eat.

He pushed his new body to his fridge. It pushed open easily enough his claws and the food inside poured onto the ground. Leftover spaghetti, old steaks, watermelon, and all the condiments. He bent down to eat the steak and swallowed it whole.

It wasn't enough. It wasn't what it wanted.

A hundred drums were pounding inside his head. They thumped and thumped, driving him towards the bedroom. He could hear his girlfriend's words through the door. She sounded so damn loud. Too damn loud.

"Hey, baby, everything okay out there? Are you feeling better? Are you ready for an after midnight session?" said Shannon.

Cody burst through the door, nearly tearing it off his hinges. Shannon screamed, but she looked good. She looked like she'd taste even better. *Must hunt. Must eat.* Every step was heavy. A thousand pounds strapped to each leg. He was headed towards the bed. Towards the woman who wouldn't stop crying. *No. Must not eat. She may be a bitch, but I can't eat her. I won't eat her. I won't eat anyone.*

The beast pushed open the door. He fled the bedroom and flew out the front door. His feet carried him faster than he'd ever moved before. The wind blew through his fur, the sky lit the earth below. He moved further from his apartment. Trees sprung up around him and he found himself in a forest. He cocked his head up at the moon. *How beautiful she looks. How lovely she is.* He could feel something happening in his body. It started from his chest and worked its way out his open snout. Cody let out a long howl. It seemed to last nearly a minute. His long ears picked up a sound. Something was close. His eyes could see well in the dark. A pack of deer weren't far away. *Must hunt. Must eat.*

The black wolf ran under the full moon.

Sanguine Sustenance

It started out as a typical night. My friends and I had gathered together for a small game of cards. Despite our young appearance we enjoyed playing poker. Max, Chris, Gary, and I had been gathering to play at Max's house for longer than we can remember. Chris hadn't arrived yet, but we decided to start without him. Gary dealt the cards and we only played a few hands before we heard the knock on the door. Max glided over, opening the door for a man to walk in that none of us recognized. None of us had invited him in. It was rude of him to walk in somewhere that he isn't welcome.

He was carrying a black sack and had an acrid odor that lingered about him. The stench sent Max back to his seat. The stranger walked over to the table where we were seated and pulled from the sack our friend's head. Blood was dripping from the neck and my stomach twitched.

He tossed Chris' head onto the ground before grabbing the cards and scattering them about the room. I quickly dropped to the floor to begin gathering all of the cards, picking them up off the ground and making sure we had a full set still. Gary ran up to the stranger to apprehend him as I was counting.

The brave action was met with a wooden bolt to the chest procured from the outsider's crossbow that he drew from his back.

Max shrieked out and flew at the stranger, but the stranger retrieved a small vial from his pocket and hurled it at Max's face. Clear liquid flowed down Max's face, melting it as he screamed in anguish. I stared up at the falling ashes that were once his face.

My friends around me were dead. I was furious. I found the strength in my stomach to confront the intruder. I was going to tear his throat out with my teeth. I ran up to him and was about to take my chance at getting revenge, but I caught a glimpse of the miniature rood around his neck and I knew better than to face this immaculate being. So I did what any self preserving creature would do, I ran away in fear.

About

Michael Polillo holds a bachelor's in journalism from Rowan University. He lives in southern New Jersey and grew up on a steady diet of kaiju movies, spaghetti westerns, and pulp books. Now he writes horror, dark comedies, and science fiction.

Other Titles

I'm Sal: The Soft Boiled Mobster – A crime thriller with mobster Sal Corbucci about his journey to find a missing daughter of a retired boxer.

The Girl with the Electric Eye – A sci-fi western with bounty hunter Ashley Morris searching for the woman who took her eye.

All titles available in paperback and ebook.

Made in the
USA
Middletown, DE